"Okay, what's g

"Nothing I can talk about."

"Why not?" Her gaze moved from his eyes to his lips, where it lingered, and then continued down his body.

That was the sexiest thing to happen to him in the past year. "I need a shower."

"Want some help?" she teased.

"Normally I'd take you up on that." He stalked across the room, pausing at the door to the bathroom.

"I was kidding. No man on earth would want to shower with me the way I must look."

He moved to the bed and leaned over her, stopping a fraction of an inch before their lips touched. "Why not? Most men I know appreciate a beautiful woman."

Those stunning hazel eyes of hers darkened. Being this close was probably a bad idea. Even if she wasn't his witness, she was injured. No way could they do anything in her condition.

But then autopilot kicked in, and Reed couldn't stop himself.

HARD TARGET

—

BARB HAN

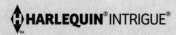

This book is dedicated to the amazing and strong people in my life.
Allison Lyons, you continue to amaze me with your insight and passion.
Jill Marsal, you are brilliant and I'm grateful to work with you.

Brandon, Jacob and Tori, you bring out the best in me every day—I love
all three of you more than you can know. John, none of this would be *this*
amazing and fun without you—my best friend and the great love of my life.

Liz Lipperman, a huge thank-you for answering my many medical
questions and offering brainstorming support. You really are the bomb!

ISBN-13: 978-0-373-69816-5

Hard Target

Copyright © 2015 by Barb Han

Recycling programs
for this product may
not exist in your area.

Printed in U.S.A.

Barb Han lives in North Texas with her very own hero-worthy husband, three beautiful children, a spunky golden retriever/standard poodle mix and too many books in her to-read pile. In her downtime, she plays video games and spends much of her time on or around a basketball court. She loves interacting with readers and is grateful for their support. You can reach her at barbhan.com.

Books by Barb Han

Harlequin Intrigue

The Campbells of Creek Bend series

Witness Protection
Gut Instinct
Hard Target

Rancher Rescue

Visit the Author Profile page at
Harlequin.com for more titles.

CAST OF CHARACTERS

Emily Baker—She's the obsession of a violent criminal. When she escapes his grasp, she's forced to depend on the good-looking cowboy border patrol agent who discovers her entering the country inside a crate full of illegal weapons.

Reed Campbell—He's the youngest Campbell brother, but that doesn't mean he's weak. In fact, he's exactly the kind of guy who puts it all on the line with every assignment, except when his heart becomes part of the mission.

Nick Campbell—The oldest Campbell, this US marshal is a phone call away when his brothers need help. He knows firsthand what it's like when one of his own goes rogue, and he'll risk everything to save his family.

Luke Campbell—He's FBI through and through but will risk his career to come to the aid of one of his family members.

Dueño—*Vicious* doesn't begin to describe this criminal with murderous tendencies and a reach across the border.

Agent Stephen Taylor—Why does he seem so willing to take Emily off Reed's hands?

Agent Cal Phillips—He disappeared from the agency after he shot Reed and left him for dead.

Agent Shane Knox—He's quick to vanish when the heat is on.

Jared—Emily's boss is a corporate "climber" but his interest in Emily seems far more personal.

Chapter One

Emily Baker pulled her legs into her chest and hugged her knees. Waves of fear and anger rolled through her.

A hammer pounded the inside of her head, a residual effect from the beatings. Her busted bottom lip was dry and cracked from dehydration.

"Move," one of the men commanded, forcing her to her feet.

A crack across her back nearly caused her to fall again.

The whole experience of the past few days had been surreal. One minute she'd been kayaking in a tropical paradise, enjoying all the rich sounds of the dense forest. The next she was being dragged through the jungle by guerrillas. She'd been blindfolded for what had to be hours, although she'd completely lost track of time, and had been led through pure hell.

Vegetation thickened the longer she'd walked. Thorns pierced her feet. The sun had blistered her skin. Ant bites covered her ankles.

A man they called Dueño had ordered the men to change her appearance. They'd chopped her hair and poured something on it that smelled like bleach. She assumed they did it to ensure she no longer matched the description of the woman the resort would report as missing. Oh, God, the word *missing* roiled her stomach.

She'd read about American tourists being snatched while on vacation, but didn't those things happen to other people? Rich people?

Not data entry clerks with no family who'd scrimped and saved for three years to take the trip in the first place.

Men in front of her fanned out, and she saw the small encampment ahead. The instant a calloused hand made contact with her shoulder, she shuddered.

"Get down!" He pushed her down on all fours.

The leader, Dueño, stood over her. He was slightly taller than the others and well dressed. His face was covered, so she couldn't pick him out of a lineup if she'd wanted to. "You want to go home, Ms. Baker?"

"Yes." How'd he know her name?

"Then tell me what I want to know. Give me the password to SourceCon." Anger laced his words.

How did he know where she worked? All thoughts of this being a random kidnapping fizzled and died.

"I can't. I don't have them." The night before she'd left for vacation, she changed them as a precaution. Her new passwords were taped to the underside of her desk at home.

"Fine. Have it your way." He turned his back. "Starve her until she talks."

Twenty-four hours tied up with no food or water had left her weak, but she couldn't give him what she didn't know.

He returned the next morning. "Do you remember them now?"

"No. I already told you I don't have them." Anger and fear engulfed her like a raging forest fire.

He backhanded her and repeated the question. When another blow didn't produce his desired result, he ordered one of the men to beat her, and another to dig a hole.

Fear gripped her as she was shoved inside the dark cramped space.

After dark, there were only three guards keeping watch. One drank until he passed out. She'd been working on loosening her bindings all day and had made progress. Maybe she could make a move to escape.

"I need to go to the bathroom."

One of the guards hauled her out of the hole, removed the rope from her ankles and then shoved her into a thicket. He looked at her with black eyes. "Two minutes."

He hadn't noticed the ropes on her arms were loose. Hope filled her chest for the first time since her capture. Immediately, she shucked the bindings from her arms, and then took off.

For two days, she'd carved her way through the dense vegetation, fearful. Any minute she'd expected the men to catch up, to stick her in another hole. Her punishment this time surely would be death.

Exhausted, feet bleeding, she made it to the edge of the jungle. In the clearing ahead, she spotted ships. Her heartbeat amplified as her excitement grew. She'd rummage around for something to eat, and then wait until dark.

Time stilled and the hours ticked by. The few berries she'd eaten kept her stomach from cramping.

When all commotion on the dock stopped, she checked manifests until she located one in English. The ship was heading to Galveston, Texas. She buried herself inside a small compartment in one of the crates. No matter how weak she was, she didn't dare sleep.

By sunrise, voices drew closer and the ship moved. The boat swayed, and she battled waves of nausea. Her stomach rumbled and churned, protesting the amount of time that had gone by without a meal.

How long had it been since she'd eaten real food? Five days? Six?

Hours had gone by and the air was becoming thicker. Her breathing labored. She swiped away a stray tear, praying she was nearing shore. All she had to do was survive a little while longer. The panels of the wooden freight box she'd jammed herself into seconds before the ship had left the dock were closing in on her, making it hard to move, or breathe. She couldn't afford another panic attack, or allow her mind to go to the place where she was in that dark hole being starved and beaten. A sob escaped before she could suppress it.

The ship had to be closing in on its destination by now. She was so close to the States she could almost taste her freedom.

Or was she?

All her hopes were riding on a journey across the Gulf of Mexico, but the truth was she could be anywhere. She reminded herself that she'd read the manifest, and prayed she'd understood it correctly.

Emily bit out a curse at the men who'd made her feel helpless and kicked at the walls of the crate, withdrawing her foot when she blistered it with another splinter. Her soles were already raw. She'd need to make sure she cleaned them up and found antibiotic ointment when she got off this horrible boat.

She'd already collected splinters in her elbows and thighs. Escaping the compound in a swimsuit wouldn't have been her first choice, but she'd grasped her first opportunity to run. There'd been no time for debate. Her chance had presented itself and she'd seized it, not stopping until long after the men's voices had faded.

She repositioned herself in the crate, grateful she could almost stretch her legs. She'd survived so far by doing mental math calculations, flexing and releasing her stomach muscles, and tightening her abs.

No food left her weak.

The minutes seemed to drip by, and her body cramped from being in such a small space. She had no watch, no cell phone and no purse.

None of which she cared about as much as her freedom.

She could get the rest once she got out of the crate and off this boat.

The resort area had been paradise when she'd first arrived, but nothing sounded better to Emily than home, a hot bath and her own bed.

Holy hell. She couldn't go home. If they knew her name and where she worked, they had to know where she lived, too. A ripple of fear skittered across already taut nerves.

She pressed her face against a crack in the crate. Darkness. Nothing but darkness behind her and darkness in front of her.

The man who'd helped her onto her kayak had told her to stay close to the ocean side and not the jungle because of the risk of running into alligators. Now she wondered if maybe they'd known about the rebel groups scouring the edges all along. They hadn't warned her about men with massive guns, and bandannas covering their faces, leaving only black eyes staring at her, coming to take her. She would've listened to that. She wouldn't have ventured off, following a monkey in the canopy. And where had the monkey gone?

Onto one of her kidnappers' shoulders.

She'd initially hoped the resort would send security once it discovered she hadn't returned to her room. She'd held on to the hope for two days in the jungle. With no shoes, her feet had been bitten, cut and aching after the daylong walks and nights of camping. And hope had retreated faster than the sun before a thunderstorm.

There'd been shouting, too. It had scared her nearly to death. At first she feared they would rape her, but no one had touched her.

Extortion? Drugs? Ransom?

Nope. None.

He'd asked for her passwords.

A sense of relief had washed over her. If she'd had to rely on her family, she'd be dead for sure. Her family wasn't exactly reliable, and they were broke. Even skilled trackers like these would have trouble locating her mother. The Bakers had split faster than an atom, and left similar devastation in their wake. At least the ones she knew.

Emily had always been the black sheep. She'd moved away, worked hard and put herself through college. Her mom had refused to allow her to take the SAT, saying it would only train her to be some corporation's slave, so she'd researched a grandfather clause in a North Texas school, did two years at a community college, and after another three years, graduated from the small university.

She'd come to North Texas solely on the promise of affordable living and an abundant job market, figuring she could build the rest of her life from there. And she had. She'd gotten a job as a data entry clerk at a computer company and was working her way up. Her boss was due a promotion and she'd been promised his job.

There were rare occasions when she heard from her mother, although it was mostly when she needed money. Turns out free love didn't pay all that much. Watching her mom wither away after her dad walked out, Emily had made a vow. No one would take away her power. Ever.

Being resourceful had gotten her through college, and landed her first real job. She'd pulled on every bit of her quick wit to escape her captors. Once back in the States, she could locate a church or soup kitchen, and get help. No way could she find a police station. Not after over-hearing her abductors talk about bribing American border police. Her body trembled. They'd hand her right back to Dueño. She'd be dead in five minutes. Not happening.

Once she was on dry land, she could figure out a way to sneak into her town house. She needed ID and clothes. There was a little money in her bank account. She could use it to disappear for a year or two. Wait it out until this whole thing blew over. Dread settled over her at the thought of leaving the only place that felt like home.

She thought about the threat Dueño had made, the underlying promise in his tone that he had every intention of delivering on his word. The way he'd said her name had caused an icy chill to grip her spine.

The ship pitched forward then stopped. Had it docked?

Emily repeated a silent protection prayer she'd learned when she was a little girl as her pulse kicked up a notch. She had no idea what she'd find on the other side of the crate.

Her skin was clammy and salty. She was starving and dehydrating. But she was alive, dammit, and she could build from there.

There were male voices. Please, let them be American. She listened intently.

At least two men shouted orders. Feet shuffled. She couldn't tell how many others there were, but at least they spoke English. Her first thought was to beat on the walls of the crate, let them find her and beg to be taken home. But then, she was in a shipment, beaten and bruised, illegally entering the country with no ID.

Would the men call police? Immigration?

There were other, worse things they could do to her when they found her, too. A full-body shiver roared through her.

She couldn't afford to risk her safety.

Besides, the man who'd had her kidnapped had been clear. She'd been his target. If she surfaced now, she'd most likely be recaptured or killed. Neither was an acceptable prospect.

Could she figure out a way to slip off the boat while the deckhands unloaded the other boxes?

If she wriggled out of the crate now, she might be seen. The only choice was to wait it out, be patient until the right opportunity presented itself. This shipment had to be loaded onto something, right? A semi? Please, not another boat.

Painful heartbeats stabbed her ribs. She tensed, coiled and prepared to spring at whatever came next.

A voice cut through the noise, and everything else went dead silent.

The rich timbre shot straight through her, causing her body to shiver in the most inappropriate way under the circumstances.

She listened more closely. There were other sounds. Feet padding and heavy breathing.

Oh, no.

Police dogs.

Their agitated barks shot through the crate like rapid gunfire, inches from Emily's face. In the small compartment, she had nowhere to hide. The dogs' heated breaths blasted through the cracks. If her odor wasn't bad enough, this certainly wouldn't help matters. Now she'd smell like dirt, sweat and bad animal breath.

Emily's heart palpitated. She prayed an officer would stop the dogs. From the sounds of them, they'd rip her to shreds.

"Hier. Komm!" another voice commanded.

Emily made out the fact the officer spoke in another language. Dutch? German?

Damn.

She was about to be exposed. Her heart clutched. She had no idea how powerful the man who'd kidnapped her was. One thing was certain. He had enough money to buy off American border police. Was she about to come face-to-face with men he had in his pocket?

She shuddered at the thought of being sent back to Dueño, to that hell.

Her left eye still burned from the crack he'd fired across her cheek when she'd told him she didn't know the codes.

Maybe she could tell the officers the truth, beg them to let her go.

If they were for real, maybe she had a chance.

Voices surrounded her. Male. Stern.

She coiled tighter, praying she'd have enough energy to fight back or run. She'd have about a half second to decide if they would send her back to that hellhole, but she wouldn't go willingly.

A side panel burst open and Emily rolled out. She popped to her feet.

The officer in front of her was tall, had to be at least six-two. His hair was almost dark enough to be black. He had intense brown eyes, and he wore a white cowboy hat. He was built long and lean with ripples of muscles. Under normal circumstances, she'd be attracted to him. But now, all she could think about was her freedom.

He had a strong jawline, and when he smiled, his cheeks were dimpled. His eyes might be intense, but they were honest, too.

She held her hands up in the universal sign of surrender. "Help me. Please. I'm American."

"You're a US citizen?" Reed Campbell had taken one look at the curled-up little ball when he opened the crate and felt an unfamiliar tug at his heart. He pushed it aside as she shot to her feet. Her face was bruised. She had a busted lip. Even though her hair was overly bleached and tangled, and she could use a shower, her hazel eyes had immense depth—the kind that drew him in, which was ridiculous under the circumstances. It had to be her vulnerability that stirred the kind of emotions that had no place at work.

"Yes." She spoke in perfect English, but American citizens didn't normally travel home in a crate from Mexico. It looked as if standing took effort. "You can sit down if you'd like."

She nodded and he helped her to a smaller crate where she eased down. He asked an agent to grab a bottled water out of his Jeep. A few seconds later, one of his colleagues produced one.

The cap was on too tight, and she seemed too weak to fight with it.

"I can do that for you." He easily twisted off the lid.

She thanked him, downed three-quarters of the bottle and then poured the rest over her face.

"What's your name?"

She stalled as though debating her answer. "Emily Baker."

"I need to see ID, ma'am. Driver's license. Passport." He looked her up and down. No way did she have a wallet tucked into her two-piece swimsuit. The material fit like an extra layer of skin, highlighting full breasts and round hips. Neither of which needed to go in his report. He forced his gaze away from the soft curves on an otherwise firm body.

He cleared his throat. Damn, dry weather.

"I don't have any with me." The words came out sharp, but the tone sounded weary and drained. The crate she was in was huge and there were several compartments. More illegals? Human trafficking? Reed had seen it all in the past six years as a Border Patrol agent.

"Let's see what else we find in here," Agent Pete Sanders said.

She seemed to realize she stood in front of them wearing next to nothing when she crossed her arms over her chest and her cheeks flushed pink. She suddenly looked even more vulnerable and small. Her embarrassment tugged at his heart. More descriptions that wouldn't go in his Homeland Security report.

She shivered, glanced down and to the right. She was about to lie. "Look. I can explain everything."

"I'm all ears."

Agents hauled over two crew members and told them to stay put.

She looked up at Reed again, and her hazel eyes were wide and fearful. Her hands shook. The men seemed to make her want to jump out of her skin even more. She was frightened, but not a flight risk. Cuffing her would most likely scare her even more. Besides, pulling her sunburned and blistered arms behind her back would hurt more than her pride. She also looked starved and dehydrated. One bottle of water would barely scratch the surface.

Getting her to talk under these circumstances might prove even more difficult. As it was, she looked too frightened to speak. Reed needed to thin her audience. He glanced at the K-9 officer. "I got this one under control. The other agents will see if there are more stashed in there. She's a quick run up to immigration."

The officer nodded before giving the command for his dog to keep searching. As soon as the two disappeared around the corner, the blonde dropped to her knees. Tears filled her eyes, a perfect combination of brown, gray and blue.

"I know how this must look. I'm not stupid. But I can explain."

"You already said that."

"Okay. Let's see. Where do I start?" Even through her fear, she radiated a sense of inner strength and independence.

Hell, he could respect that. Even admired her for it. But allowing a suspected illegal alien, or whatever she was, entry into the country wasn't his call. "At the beginning. How'd you end up in the crate?"

"I, uh, I…"

This was going nowhere. He wanted to reach out to her, help her, but she had to be willing to save herself. "We have some folks you can talk to. They can help."

"No. Please don't take me anywhere else. Just let me go. I'll show up to whatever court date. I won't disappear. I promise. I have a good job. One that I can't afford to lose."

Reed knew desperation. Hell, most drug runners were just as desperate. They'd offer bribes, their women, pretty much anything to manipulate the system.

His sixth sense told him this was different. There was an innocence and purity to her eyes that drew him in. Victim?

He pressed his lips into a frown. "Let's not get ahead of ourselves."

"Am I under arrest?"

"No."

"Then I'm free to go?" The flash of hope in her eyes seared his heart.

"I didn't say that." With her perfect English, he knew she wasn't illegal. But what else would she be doing tucked in a crate headed for the States, looking like a punching bag? Human trafficking? She was battered and bruised. If someone was trying to sell her, she'd fought back. But that explanation didn't exactly add up. Most traffickers didn't risk damaging the "product."

The officers moved to another wall on the other side of the crate. Twenty people could've been stuffed in there. He hoped like hell they weren't about to open up the other side and find more in the same shape as her. Seeing a woman beaten up didn't do good things to Reed. He fisted his hands.

"What happened to you?" Even bruised and dirty,

she was pretty damn hot. The tan two-piece she wore
stretched taut against full breasts. Reed refocused on
her heart-shaped face. Was someone trying to sell her
into the sex trade? One look at her curves and long silky
legs told him men would pay serious money for her. His
protective instincts flared at the thought.

"I was on vacation and was robbed. They stole my
passport. Said if I told authorities, they'd find me and
kill me. I spent a night in the jungle trying to find my
way back to the resort. I walked for an eternity, saw this
ship and hopped on board praying no one would follow,
find or catch me."

The bruises on her face and body outlined the fact
she wasn't being honest. He shot her a sideways glance.
"What happened to your face?"

"One of the men hit me?" Yeah, she was digging—
digging a hole she might not be able to climb out of. It
would take more than that to cause the bruising she had.

"I hope I don't have to remind you it's not in your best
interest to lie to the law."

Her gaze darted around before settling on him.

"So, the story you're sticking with is that they jumped
you on the beach?"

"No. I went into town."

"In just your swimsuit?"

A red rash crawled up her neck. Hell, he hadn't meant
to embarrass her. She already seemed uncomfortable as
hell in his presence. He had an extra shirt in his vehicle
he could give her.

"Oh, right. I, uh, I already said I got lost."

"Enough to jump inside a random cargo ship and go
wherever it took you? Sounds like someone trying to get

away from something." Or someone. Yet another truth that hit him like a sucker punch.

She fixed her gaze on the cement. Was she about to lie again?

"You want to explain what really happened?" he preempted, pulling a notebook and pen from his pocket. She was beautiful. An inappropriate attraction surged through him. He shouldn't have passed on the offer of sex from Deanna the other night. And yet, the thrill of sex for sex's sake had never appealed to Reed.

"I've been through a lot in the past couple of days. Like I said, I got disoriented or something." She blinked against the bright sun. "Where am I?"

"Galveston, Texas."

Relief washed over her desperate expression. "Oh, thank God. That's perfect. I'm from Plano, a Dallas suburb."

"I'm familiar with the area. Have family there." He looked up from his pad. "What are you really doing here?"

"I work for a company called SourceCon. You can call and check. They'll tell you I'm on vacation. My boss has my itinerary."

Finally, he was getting somewhere. She was still lying about getting lost in Mexico, and she was a bad liar, too. That was a good sign. Meant she didn't normally lie her way out of situations. She didn't have the convictions of a pathological liar. But now he had something to work with. It wouldn't take much to make a quick call to verify her employment. He could do that for her, at least.

The sound of one of the crate's other walls smacking the pavement split the air.

"Hey, Campbell," Pete said.

"Yeah. Right here."

"You're gonna want to see this." He rounded the corner, hoisting an AR-15 in the air. "Looks like your friend here is involved in running guns."

Reed deadpanned her. "You just bought yourself a ride to Homeland Security."

Chapter Two

The trouble Emily was in hit with the force of a tsunami. "I'm broke. I'm exhausted. And they promised to hunt me down and kill me if I crossed them."

A strong hand pulled her to her feet.

"You can lean on me," he said before turning his head and shouting for someone to bring water.

The agent's gaze skimmed her face one more time, pausing at her busted lip. His brilliant brown eyes searched for the truth. A thousand butterflies released in her stomach with him so close.

Emily hadn't seen a mirror, but based on her amount of pain she had to be a total mess. The only good news was that he seemed to be considering what she was saying. *Please. Please. Please. Believe me.*

Another bottle of water arrived. The agent twisted off the cap and handed it to her. His broad cheekbones and rich timbre set off a sparkler inside her.

The glorious water cooled her still-parched throat. She downed most of the contents, using the leftovers to splash more water on her face. "Thank you."

Her stomach growled. "Any chance you have a hamburger hidden somewhere?"

He shot her a look full of pity. Something else flashed

behind his brown eyes when he said, "We can stop and pick something up on the way."

"Please don't turn me in. I can prove I'm American if I can get to my belongings." She took a step forward, and her knees buckled.

The agent caught her before she hit the ground. "Let's get something in your stomach first."

He helped her across the loading dock to his Jeep parked in the lot.

She eased onto the passenger seat.

"You're welcome to my extra shirt." He produced a white button-down from the back. "And I have a couple extra bottles of water and a towel."

A spark of hope lit inside her. Was he going to help? She thanked him for the supplies, pouring the opened bottle of water onto the towel first. The wet cloth felt cool on her skin. She dabbed her face before wiping her neck, chest and arms.

Pulling on the shirt required a little more finesse. She winced as she stretched out her arms. The agent immediately made a move to help. He eased one of her hands in the sleeve, and then the other. She managed the buttons on her own. Taking in a breath, the smell of his shirt reminded her of campfires lit outdoors and clean spring air.

"I have a power bar. Keep a few in a cooler in back for those long stretches of nothingness when I'm patrolling fence." He held out the wrapped bar and another water.

She took both, placed the water in her lap and tried to steady her hands enough to open the wrapper.

The protein bar tasted better than steak. She drained the water bottle in less than a minute. "I've already thanked you, but I'd like to repay you somehow."

His gaze locked onto hers. "Tell me the truth about

what happened to you. I can't stop these men from hurting other women without information."

Was he saying what she thought? The men who'd abducted her belonged to a kidnapping ring? Of course they did. She hadn't even considered it before, she'd been too concerned about her own life, but they seemed practiced and professional. If she could stop them, she had to try.

She nodded.

He climbed into the driver's side, put the key in the ignition and then waited.

"At first, I couldn't believe what was happening to me. I just kept thinking this couldn't be real." She looked over at him, hating that she was trembling with fear. "I was dragged through the jungle for hours, starved and then stuck in a hole with no food or water." Tears welled. She would hold back the information about knowing she'd been a target until she was certain she could trust him. As it was, maybe he'd let her go.

"Do you know how long you were there?"

"What day is it?"

He glanced at his watch. "Monday."

"My flight arrived in Mexico last Monday."

"A week ago."

"The sky was clear blue, the most beautiful shade I've ever seen. I'd stayed up late at a welcome party, so I didn't get outside until noon or so the next day. Took a kayak out, and that's when they grabbed me."

Compassion warmed his stern features. "Now we're getting somewhere. How many men were there?"

"Half a dozen."

"Can you give a description?"

"They wore bandannas to cover their faces. Other than that, they were a little taller than me." She was five foot seven. "They had to be five-eight or five-nine. Black hair and eyes."

His face muscles tensed.

"I just described half of the country, didn't I?"

He nodded, his expression radiating a sense of calm. "Dark skin or light?"

"Dark. Definitely dark."

"Can you describe their clothing?"

"Most of them wore old jeans and faded T-shirts. Looked like secondhand stuff. They were dirty."

"Some guerrilla groups live in the jungle," he agreed.

Did he believe her? He'd stopped looking at her as if she belonged in the mental ward, so that had to be a good sign.

"If they abducted you for extortion, they would've contacted your family. Can I call someone? A spouse?"

"I'm not married." An emotion she couldn't identify flashed behind the agent's brown eyes. "As for the rest of my family… There's not really… It's complicated."

"Mother? Father?"

"I don't know where he is. My mom isn't reachable. She's sick." Why was she suddenly embarrassed by her dysfunctional family?

The better question might be when had she not been?

Emily remembered being scared to death she wouldn't pass the background check required to work in her job for a major computer company. She'd had to get clearance since she entered data for various banks, some of which came from foreign interests. With a mom living in basically a cult and a dad who was MIA, Emily had feared she wouldn't get through the first round with her prospective employer. Emily had always been responsible. She hadn't even sampled marijuana in college as so many of her friends had. While all her classmates were "experimenting" and partying, she'd been working two jobs to pay tuition and make rent. Not that she was a saint. She just didn't have spare time or energy to do anything besides work, study and sleep.

She had to keep a decent GPA, which didn't leave a lot of time for anything else.

Heck, her college boyfriend had left her because she'd been too serious. He'd walked out, saying he wanted to be with someone more fun.

What was that?

Life hadn't handed Emily "fun." It had given her a deserter for a dad and a mom who was as sweet as she was lost.

Fun?

Emily clamped down a bitter laugh.

She'd had fun about as often as she'd had sex in the past year. And that really was a sad statement. Getting away, going to the beach, was supposed to represent a big step toward claiming her future and starting a new life.

"There's no one we can call?" The agent's voice brought her back to the present.

She shook her head. There was one name she could give him, her boss. She hated to do it. The last thing she wanted to do was jeopardize her job, but Jared could corroborate her story and then the agent would believe her. Possibly even let her go?

With the information she'd given the agent so far, she had a feeling she was going to need all the help she could get. "My boss."

Agent Campbell pulled his cell from his pocket.

She gave him Jared's number and took a deep breath.

REED PUNCHED IN the number the witness had given while he kept one eye on her.

She was still desperate, and there was an off chance she'd do something stupid, like run. He didn't feel like chasing after her. He'd catch her. And then they'd be having a whole different conversation about her immediate future.

As it was, he figured a quick trip to Homeland Security would be all that was required. Minimal paperwork. Let them sort out the rest.

His years on the job told him she wasn't a hard-core criminal. There was something about her situation, her, that ate at his insides. God help him.

"This is Jared," came through the cell. His voice was crisp, and he sounded young. Early thirties.

Reed identified himself as a Border Patrol agent. "I'm calling to verify employment."

"Then you'll want to speak to HR."

"I'd rather talk to you if it's possible," Reed interjected.

"That's against policy—"

"I wouldn't ask if it wasn't a matter of national security. You can clear something up for me. Save me a lot of time going through rigmarole, sir." Reed listened for the telltale signs he'd convinced Jared.

A deep sigh came across the line.

Bingo. "Does Emily Baker work for you?"

"Yes, she does. Why? Is she all right?"

Reed picked up on the uncomfortable note in Jared's voice. Was it curiosity or something more? "Is she there today?"

"No. She's on vacation. Mexico, I think."

Part of her story matched up. The woman sitting beside him could be anyone, though. He'd already caught her glimpsing his gun. Logic told him she was debating whether or not to make a run for it.

"Can you give me a description of Miss Baker?"

"Why? Did something happen to her?" Panic raised his tone an octave. Something told Reed the guy on the phone was interested in more than her work performance. Wasn't he the caring boss? A twinge of jealousy shot through him. What was that all about?

She was vulnerable. Reed's protective instincts jumped into overdrive. He was reacting as he would if this was one of his sisters, he told himself.

"No. Nothing to worry about, sir. Routine questions." Reed hadn't exactly lied. She was a witness.

"Okay. Good. Um, let's see. She's medium height, thin, light brown hair. She's a runner, so, um, she has the build for it, if you know what I mean."

"Yeah. I get the reference." How nice that her boss paid attention to her workout routine. Clearly, there was more to this story. An office affair? Disappointment settled over Reed for reasons he couldn't explain. Why did he care whom she dated?

He reminded himself to focus on the case. This woman fit two-thirds of the description. It was obvious her hair had been bleached. The dye job was bad, and so was the cut. Her hair had been chopped off. Even so, she was beautiful.

And her legs were long and toned. She could be a runner. He made a mental note of the fact, in case she decided to bolt. It was easy to see she was in good physical condition, aside from events of the past few days.

She glanced around, antsy. Her expression set, determined, as she skimmed the docks. Was she working with someone? For someone?

Or was she just a few grains of sand short of a castle?

The tougher job was to assess her mental fitness. If she wasn't involved in bringing guns into the country, and, really and truly, she would've been smart enough to have one loaded at the ready if she was, he had to consider the possibility she might be a danger to herself or others.

He'd witnessed all kinds of crazy.

In fact, in six years with Border Patrol, he'd seen just about everything. And a whole lot of nothing, too, especially when he was a rookie.

"Eye color?"

"Green, I think."

They were hazel, but lots of people confused hazel with green or blue. The description was close enough. "Thank you, sir. That clears everything up."

"She'll be back to work next Monday, right?"

Reed figured the boss wanted the answer to his question more for personal reasons than anything else. "I don't see why not."

"And she's okay? You're sure?"

Another sprig of jealousy sprouted. "She is. That's all the information I need. Have a nice—"

"I don't want to ask anything inappropriate, but our job requires a certain level of security clearance. She hasn't gone and done anything that might jeopardize her position at work, has she?"

"Why would she do that?" Reed knew she wasn't telling him something, but he doubted she was involved in criminal activity. Couldn't rule it out yet. Even though his instincts never lied, he preferred logic and evidence.

Did this whole episode have to do with her job? What would she have to gain?

A relieved sigh came across the line. "She wouldn't. At least, I don't think she would. I guess you can never really tell about people, but I don't have to tell you that. Not in your line of work."

The man finally said something smart. "Desperate people can do all kinds of interesting things."

"I'm sure. I already asked, but she's okay, right?"

"Yeah. She'll be back to work next week, and I'm sure she'll explain everything then." Reed ended the call.

"I lost my job, didn't I?" She sounded defeated. "It doesn't matter."

"You didn't tell me everything," he hedged.

She repositioned in her seat.

"You're tired and hungry, so I'm afraid you're going to make a bad choice. Whatever you're running from, I can help you."

She deadpanned him. "No. You can't."

"Not if you don't tell me what it is."

"I won't run. Please don't take me in." Her wide hazel eyes pleaded.

"There's protocol for situations like these. You came into the country in a shipment full of guns. Who do they belong to?"

"I'd tell you if I knew." Tears welled in her eyes.

"I need a name. They'll take it easy on you if you co-operate."

"Are you arresting me?" She glanced toward the field to her right.

Was she getting ready to make her move?

He started the engine, determined to keep her from

making another mistake she'd regret. "Buckle up. We can finish this conversation over a burger."

"You didn't answer my question. Are you going to arrest me?" she repeated slowly, as if he was dim.

"No. Why? Do you plan on giving me a reason to?"

The drive to the nearest fast-food burger place was quiet. His passenger closed her eyes and laid her head back.

She didn't open them when he pulled into the drive-through lane and ordered two burgers, two fries and two milkshakes at the speaker box.

Reed gripped the steering wheel tighter, thinking about what she'd been through in the past few days. He also realized she was keeping secrets. Professional curiosity had him wanting to find out what they were. Or was it something else?

He dismissed the idea as standing in the sun too long back at the docks. His interest in Emily Baker was purely professional.

At this point, he'd classify her as a witness. However, she was walking a fine line of being moved into another category—suspect—and she didn't want to be there. He should probably haul her up to Homeland Security and be done.

But he couldn't.

Something in those hazel eyes told him there was a bigger story, one that frightened her to the point of almost becoming mute.

If she talked, he might be able to track down gun runners, or get the connection he needed to stop another coyote from dumping illegals across the border. Heck, most died of dehydration before they ever reached their desired location. She was weak. No way was she illegal, but they used the same paths for everything from human trafficking to gun running. Besides, maybe she had information that could help him make a bust. The innocence and desperation in her voice had drawn him in. He needed to make sure she'd be okay.

He couldn't turn his back on her any more than he could walk away from one of his sisters. Something about Emily brought out a similar protective instinct, but that's where the similarities ended. Nothing else about her reminded him of his siblings.

After paying at the window, he accepted the food. There was a shady spot in the parking lot across the street. He pulled into it and parked.

She blinked her eyes open when he cut off the engine.

He unwrapped a burger and handed it to her. "It's not steak, but it should help with your hunger."

Her eyes lit up as she took the offering. "That smells nothing short of amazing."

A few bites into her meal, she set her burger down. "I don't understand. I'm famished but I can't finish it."

Poor thing was starving. Another fact in this case that made Reed want to punch something.

It was one thing for traffickers and drug pushers to maim and kill each other, but to drag women and children into their web made his fists clench and his jaw muscle tick. Five minutes alone with any one of them, and he'd leave his badge and gun outside the door.

"That was the best food I've ever had," she said, wiping her mouth with a napkin. "Ouch. Sorry. I'm bleeding again." She searched the empty food bag and seemed to fight back tears. "You've been really nice to me and I don't want to get blood on your clean white shirt."

"Nothing to worry about." Reed handed her his napkin. "It's an old shirt. A little blood won't hurt anything."

Her back was ramrod. He wasn't any closer to getting her to trust him.

Maybe softening his approach would work. "Believe me when I say I've had to clean up worse than that. The shirt's yours. Keep it."

She apologized again. Her bottom lip quivered, indicating she was probably on the brink of losing it. Who could blame her? She'd been amazingly strong so far.

For now, the person of interest in his passenger seat was safe and calm. She'd had a few minutes to think about where she might end up if she didn't give him something to work with. "Why'd they really hit you?"

She searched nearby shrubs and buildings as if expecting the men who'd hurt her to jump out from behind one.

Fear was a powerful tool.

Whoever hurt her did a good job of making her believe he'd come back for more if she gave him up. "I know this is tough. Believe me. But it's the only way I can help you."

She brought her hands up to rub her temples and trained her gaze on the patch of cement in front of the Jeep. She was teetering on the edge.

He was getting close to a breakthrough. "They shouldn't be allowed to get away with this. I don't care what they threatened. The US government is bigger than whoever did this to you."

A few tears fell, streaking her cheeks.

"Whatever they said, don't believe them."

She dropped her hands to her lap, and then turned toward him. Her hazel eyes pierced right through him. "You give me your personal promise to protect me?"

Chapter Three

If Agent Campbell made one wrong blink, Emily had already decided she'd bolt. She'd put it out there and asked him to make a commitment. Now it was his turn to make a move.

"It's my job to—"

"I want to know if you promise to protect me. And not just because of your badge." Even though he was a stranger, everything about the agent next to her said he was a man of his word. If he made a personal pledge, she'd trust him a little.

He finished chewing his bite of hamburger and swallowed before he set his food on the wrapper and used a napkin to clean his hands.

"My name is Reed, and you have my word." He stuck his hand out between them.

She took it, knowing she shouldn't. There was no way he could guarantee her safety. The instant they'd made contact, a spark ran between them. She didn't withdraw her hand. Neither did he.

Their eyes locked, and she felt another jolt. An underlying sexual current simmered between them, which was shocking given what she'd been through. He was the first person in ages who'd expressed interest in helping and protecting her, she reasoned, and it felt nice to have that.

Under different circumstances, she might enjoy the spark. Not now. All she could think about was getting out of this mess and going into hiding.

Another thing was certain. By the set of his jaw, she could tell that Reed Campbell meant what he said. No doubt about it. Could he deliver against a rebel faction that could have law enforcement officers bought and paid for?

He looked like the kind of man who, once he gave his word, would die trying to deliver on his commitments. And something about the depths of his eyes had her wanting to move a little closer toward his strength, his light.

All her danger signals flared.

Getting too close to a man who could have her locked up was a bad idea, no matter how much honesty radiated from his brown eyes.

His cell buzzed, and she pulled her hand back, breaking their grasp.

A half-eaten burger sat on his knee on top of the wrapper. He answered the call, keeping his gaze on her.

Was he afraid she'd take off? He had to know she'd scatter like a squirrel at one loud noise.

At six-two with muscles for days, he must realize he could be physically intimidating. Was that why he seemed to make so much of an effort to keep her calm?

Against her better judgment, it was working. She felt a sense of being protected with him near. A luxury she couldn't afford.

"Uh-huh, I have her right here," he said. His gaze narrowed.

Trouble?

"Thanks, but I've got this one."

Was someone offering to take her off his hands? This seemed out of the blue. No way could it be standard procedure.

A shudder of fear roared through her. She folded her arms to stave off the chill skittering across her skin.

"No, I'm sure." He shook his head as if for emphasis. "We're heading northbound on I-45. Why?"

Emily's chest squeezed, and she knew something was wrong. Agent Campbell gave the person on the phone the wrong location. Why would he do that?

"Will do." Agent Campbell ended his call.

"Who was that?"

He sat looking dumbfounded for a second. "That was odd. Agent Stephen Taylor volunteered to meet me and take you off my hands. Said he was headed in and it wouldn't be any trouble to take you along with him."

"I don't know this area at all, but we're sitting in a parking lot, and you told him we were on the highway. Why?"

Using the paper wrap, he wadded up the few bites of hamburger he had left and tossed it in the bag. "That call doesn't sit right. Something's off."

Emily gasped. "That can't be normal."

"Nope. Never happened to me before in six years of service." He checked his rearview mirror.

The last thing Emily wanted to do was tell the agent more about what had happened to her. In fact, she'd like to be able to forget it altogether. But both of their lives were in danger now, and he deserved to know the risk he was taking. "There was a man back in Mexico. They called him Dueño. He promised to…"

Saying the words out loud proved harder than she expected. Tears pricked the backs of her eyes.

Gray clouds rolled in from the coast as the winds picked up speed.

The agent sat quietly, hands resting on the steering wheel, giving her the space she needed to find the courage to tell him the rest.

"To find me no matter what. I know he has law enforcement on his payroll. I overheard them talking about it."

Agent Campbell started the ignition, and eased the Jeep into traffic. "They give any names?"

His rich timbre was laced with anger. She could imagine how an honest man like him would take it personally if one of his own was on the take. "No. All I knew was that once I got away from him, I had to disappear. I couldn't trust law enforcement or anyone else. That's why I can't let you take me in. I'm begging you to let me go."

Thunder rumbled in the distance.

"Hate to believe agents are on the take." He looked to be searching his memory as he narrowed his gaze onto the stretch of road in front of them. He muttered a string of curse words. "There have been a few articles in the paper hinting at the possibility. The department issued a warning. We'd picked up a few bad eggs during a hiring surge, but we've been assured they were weeded out."

"You take me in and he'll get to me. He has people on the inside. I can identify him and testify. They'll kill me."

"Slow down. I'm not going to let that happen. We can figure this out."

"They won't stop until they find me."

"Which is why it's a bad idea for me to let you go. At least while you're with me, I can protect you."

"Can't you tell your department you let me go?"

"Why would I do that?"

"Because you have to. I know what they wanted when they targeted me. There's a fortune on the line."

"Hold on a sec. You led me to believe this was random," he said. His eyes flashed anger.

"I'm sorry. I lied. I wasn't sure if I could trust you before." She had to now.

His grip on the steering wheel tightened. His gaze intensified. "What else?"

"They wanted my passwords. I work at a computer company. We keep account information secure for big banking institutions. I'm sure they planned on moving money."

"Cybercrime can be harder to track if they know what they're doing. Why didn't you just give them the passwords and save yourself?"

She deadpanned him. "I figured they'd kill me either way. Even so, I couldn't give them passwords if I'd wanted to. I always change them before I leave for vacation. I didn't have my new ones memorized."

"He beat you because he didn't believe you."

"Not for a second."

"I'm assuming you have your codes written down somewhere?"

She nodded. A thought struck her. "What if they get to my place and find them? I'm sure they knew where I lived."

Agent Campbell's cell buzzed again. He put on his turn signal, moved into the left turn lane and then shot a glance at her before answering. He turned on his hazard lights, even though there were no cars coming.

Thunder rumbled louder. A storm was coming.

"Yes, sir, I heard from the agent."

There was a long pause.

"No, I didn't turn over the witness. I can run her in to make a statement."

Emily slipped her hand as close to the seat belt release button as she could without drawing attention. Her pulse kicked up a notch.

A light rain started, nothing more than a spring shower. The glorious liquid spotted the windshield.

She had enough sustenance in her to manage a good sprint. Would it be enough to get away? Her feet still ached and her head pounded. A good night of sleep, some medicine, and she'd recover. But would her body give her what she needed to get away now?

Possibilities clicked through her mind.

If she made a run for it, could she disappear in the neighboring subdivision? Maybe hide in a parked car?

The capable agent in the seat next to her would catch her. His muscled thighs said he could outrun her if he needed to. One look at the ripple of muscles underneath his shirtsleeve said he was much stronger than she.

Might be a risk she'd have to take.

Stay there and she'd be dead in an hour if he followed through with his plans to take her to Homeland Security. One of the men in Dueño's pocket would alert him to her whereabouts, and they'd be ready for her when she walked outside.

The best chance she had would be to make a move right now while Agent Campbell was distracted by his phone call. If she were smart, she'd unbuckle and run like hell.

"I didn't say she was a suspect, sir."

Her heart jackhammered in her chest. Should she bolt?

REED GLANCED OVER at Emily. Her back was stiff, her breathing rapid and shallow. He covered her hand with his, and she relaxed a little. A smile quirked the corner of his lip.

"I can take this one, sir. Not a problem."

Confident he'd convinced his boss, Reed ended the call. A rogue agent was a dangerous thing. Reed could personally attest to that.

This one had involved his boss, who was being played. The agent who'd tried to get his hands on Emily wouldn't be allowed to have his way.

"Your boss wanted you to hand me over to someone else, didn't he?"

Reed nodded.

"Could going against your boss cost your job?"

He wasn't sure why he chuckled. "Yeah."

"You're willing to take that risk to help me?"

"It's my duty." "Honor First" was more than words on a page to Reed.

Emily leaned against the seat and pinched the bridge of her nose. "Then, what do we do next?"

"Good question."

Reed checked the rearview and saw a truck screaming toward them.

He banked a U-turn in time to see a metal shotgun barrel aimed at them.

Emily must've seen it, too, because she yelped.

"Get down on the floorboard. Now."

A *boom* split the air.

Reed gunned the gas pedal, made a U-turn and then hooked a right, blazing through the empty parking lot. For a split second, time warped and the memory of being shot and left for dead blitzed him.

A walk down Memory Lane would have to wait. He battled against the heavy thoughts, blocking them out. If he lived, *correction*, when he got them out of this mess, he'd deal with those. *Yeah, right, like that's going to happen.*

The reality was that he'd had plenty of time since returning to work to rationalize his feelings. Doing that ranked about as high on his list as shoveling cow manure out of the barn at Gran's place. He took that back. Shoveling cow manure was far more appealing.

Reed glanced at Emily, who was not more than a ball in the floorboard. Her face scrunched in pain from being forced to move. The thought of doubling her agony lanced his chest. "Hang tight. I'll get us to safety soon."

She glanced at him through fearful hazel eyes. "Maybe we should break up. I can hide on my own. Might be better now that they know we're together."

Was she still worried he'd run her in? Handing her over to his agency would only put her in more jeopardy. "Not a chance."

Anxiety and fear played across her features.

A need to protect Emily surged, catching Reed off guard, because it ran deeper than his professional oath. He knew exactly what it was like to be in her position—to be the target of someone who had a dirty agent in their pocket. Reed had a bullet hole in his back to prove it.

"I'm your best option right now. And I'm not ready to let you out of my sight."

Chapter Four

Pain rippled through Emily's bruised and battered body as she crouched low and hugged her knees into her chest, making herself as small as possible in the floorboard. One of her ribs had to be cracked. The sharp pain in her chest sliced through her thoughts. Being run through a cheese grater would hurt less than the bruises on her face and body.

The agent, Reed, had said she could trust him. He'd said the magic words—he wasn't hauling her butt in to Homeland Security. And yet, her internal alarm system was still set to red alert. Why? What was it about him that had her wanting to run? Was it the alarming comfort his presence brought?

Sporadic turns and the sound of another shotgun blast said they still had company. Emily didn't dare try to peek even though her tightly coiled nerves might break at any moment if she didn't know what was happening. Even so, she doubted her body would be able to respond to her brain's command to get up.

Reed swerved the car left and then made a hard right. "Wish I'd been alone when I found you. That would make things less complicated."

"Would you have believed me?"

His compressed frown said it all. No, he wouldn't have. "I owe you an apology for that."

"I don't blame you. I'm sure you deal with all kinds of crazy people in your work."

"Most have nothing to lose when they run into me. And I've learned logic is a better resource than instinct."

He was used to being shot at? That revelation shouldn't reassure her. Oddly enough, that's exactly what it did. Maybe because she had no clues how to escape armed men or dodge bullets and there was no way she'd still be alive without his expertise. Her world had been catapulted into a whole new stratosphere of danger. Having a man around who knew how to use a gun and was on her side didn't seem like the worst thing that could happen.

Yet, depending on anyone was foreign to her. Thoughts of too many hours of her childhood spent crouched low in the corner behind her bed while her mother experienced "free love" in the next room assaulted Emily. She'd been old enough to remember what it was like to live in a suburb with a normal family and a father whom she believed loved her. Her fairy-tale world had ended the day he left. Emily squeezed her eyes tighter, trying to block out the memory.

Emily slowly counted to a hundred to keep her mind busy, refusing to let fear seize her when more bullets came at them. They pinged by her head tat-tat-tat style, and she knew by the sound difference that whoever was chasing them had changed weapons.

"I can lose them around this bend or when I get on this highway. This turn is going to get hairy, so hang on."

Chancing a glance at Reed, seeing someone who wasn't afraid, held her nerves a notch below panic. However, the contents of her stomach retaliated at the high rate of speed combined with sharp turns. She'd probably eaten too fast because the burger and milkshake churned. "Are they still back there?"

"Get back in the seat belt. The threat has tripled, and we're going to sustain a hit." The authority in his voice sent a trill of worry through her.

"Okay." She struggled to move, wincing as she planted one hand on the glove compartment and the other on the seat, praying she could gain enough leverage to push herself up from her awkward position on the floorboard. Her arms gave out and she landed hard, racking up another bruise on her hip.

A glance at Reed said they were almost out of time.

"Brace yourself for impact." He tapped the brake and swerved.

Emily lurched forward, her head caught by Reed's right hand moments before it hit the dash. Pushing through the pain, she pressed up to the seat and quickly fastened the belt over her shoulder.

Large SUVs pulled on each side of them as the truck she recognized from earlier roared up from behind.

The quick look Reed shot her next said whatever was about to happen wasn't going to be good. He floored the gas pedal, shooting out front. Temporarily.

On the right, the SUV hit the brakes. The one on the left barreled beside them, keeping pace.

The window of opportunity to hop onto the freeway and lose these guys was closing with the SUV on the left blocking the on-ramp.

A bumper crunched against the back of the Jeep. Emily's head whipped forward.

Dueño's reach had long arms. Just as he had promised. Could Emily envision a life on the run? No. She'd fought too hard to put down roots. She'd found a new city, bought a town house and worked her butt off to be next in line for her boss's job. Dueño was forcing her into a different direction. Anger burned through her.

Another hard jerk of the steering wheel and Emily felt herself tumbling, spinning.

Reed's rich timbre penetrated the out-of-control Ferris wheel. "Relax as much as you can."

Time temporarily suspended. Emily drifted out of her own body as the spinning slowed, and then stopped.

Everything went black, but she still could hear shouting. Someone was yelling at her. A deeply masculine voice called. She coughed and blinked her eyes open.

Smoke was everywhere.

Everything burned. Her nose. Her eyes. Her throat.

Her body might've stopped spinning, but her head hadn't.

"Emily. Stay with me." The voice came from a tunnel filled with light.

Or did it?

There was something comforting about the large physical presence near her.

"Emily. I need you to try to move." A sense of urgency tinged the apologetic tone.

Her response came out as a croak. She tried harder to open her eyes and gain her bearings.

Sirens sounded in the distance a few moments after she heard another pop of gunfire. The men. Oh, no. All at once she remembered being on the run. Their car had been forced off the road, while speeding, and thrown into a dangerous spin. The Jeep had rolled. And that voice calling her belonged to Border Patrol Agent Reed Campbell.

Her eyes shot open.

Heat from a fire blazed toward her. Flames licked at her skin. Thick smoke filled her lungs.

She was trapped in a burning car while men shot at her. It took another few precious seconds for her to realize she was upside down. At least the inferno kept the men at bay, except for Reed. He was right by her side. An unfamiliar feeling stuck in her chest at the thought someone actually had her back for a change. Emily wanted to gravitate toward the pleasant emotion, except she couldn't move. She wiggled her hips, hoping to break free. No luck.

The seat belt must be stuck.

There was no feeling in her legs. She tamped down panic, knowing full well that couldn't be good. Even if she could work the belt free, which she was trying with both hands, how would she run?

She'd have to solve that puzzle when she came to it.

"Take this." A shiny metal object was being thrust at her through the thick wall of smoke separating her from the agent.

Reed's face was covered in ashes and worry lines. Blood dripped down his cheek from a cut on his forehead. There was compassion in his clear brown eyes and what appeared to be fear.

She took the offering, a knife.

"Cut yourself free." His arms cradled her shoulders.

"Okay." She shot him a scared look.

"I'll catch you. I won't let you get hurt."

Her gaze widened at the figure moving toward them. "Behind you."

The agent turned and fired his weapon.

She worked the knife against the fabric, wanting to be ready, knowing they were out of time.

Sirens split the air.

Reed turned his attention back to her as soon as the man disappeared. "I'm ready. Go."

The last patch of thread cut easily. Emily didn't want to think about how good his hands felt on her as he pulled her from the burning Jeep across the hard, unforgiving earth. Or how nice it was to have someone in her corner.

The head of the House believed placing labels on people degraded them, so he simply called her girl. Her mom soon followed his lead.

Growing up in a house full of free love and short on anything meaningful, like her mother's laughter, had made Emily wary and distrustful of people. Watching her mom adopt the long hair and threadbare clothes everyone in the House wore made Emily feel even more distanced from everything familiar.

In the twelve years Emily had lived there, her mom had six children by various housemates. It had been like living in a time warp. Apparently, the label "Father" was also degrading because no one stepped up to help care for the little ones, save for Emily. She'd taken care of the children until one of the men had decided that at seventeen she was old enough to learn about free love. She'd fought back, escaped and then ran.

Emily had learned quickly the outside world could be harsh, too.

With no friends on the streets, she'd had to fight off men who confused her homelessness for prostitution. Her first stroke of luck had come when she found a flier for a shelter that handed out free breakfast. A worker there had told her about the nearby shelter for teens. For the first time since leaving Texas as a child, Emily had her own room.

All her life savings, money she'd made from her job at the local movie theater, was hidden in the House. Emily had saved every penny. Needing a fresh start, she'd slipped into the House, took her life savings and then bought a bus ticket to Dallas, where she could return home and put down roots.

By the time she'd finished a few college courses and gotten a decent job, her half siblings had scattered across the country, and she heard from her mother mostly when she needed something.

No matter how honest and pure the agent looked, Emily knew not to get too comfortable.

Feeling vulnerable out in the open, she searched for the men. Where were they?

She glanced around, half expecting more gunfire. Instead, EMTs ran toward them and all she could hear was the glorious thunder of their footsteps.

But, where was Reed?

Then she saw him. He lay flat on his back and her chest squeezed when she saw how much blood soaked his shirt. One set of EMTs rushed to him, blocking her view. Another went to work on her as firemen put out the blaze.

The cavalry had arrived.

But how long before Dueño's men returned to finish the job?

Emily needed a plan.

Heaven knew she could never rely on her mother. The woman had shattered when Emily's father left. Even then, Emily knew she needed to help her mother. The woman couldn't do much for herself in the broken state she was in. When she'd finally forced herself out of bed, a neighbor introduced her to "a new way of thinking."

It wasn't long before Emily's mom packed the pair of them up and moved to California to live in the House. Emily had been excited about the promise of perpetual sunshine, but her enthusiasm was short-lived when she figured out no one ever left the grounds except in groups to shop for food.

Which was why she couldn't afford to rely on the agent much longer. Especially not the way he stirred confusing feelings inside her that had no business surfacing. She knew where that would end up.

REED STRIPPED OFF the oxygen mask covering his face. "I'm fine."

"Can you tell me what day it is?" the young EMT asked.

"Monday. And I know I've been in an accident. I was forced off the road by another vehicle. I have to call local police to file a report." He reached for his phone, needing an excuse to step away and make eye contact with Emily. He wanted to know she'd be okay. Men were huddled around her, working on her. Reed tamped down the unexpected jolt of anxiety tensing his shoulders. "What's going on with my witness? She'll be okay, right?"

"We'll know in a few minutes."

Not good enough. Reed had to know now. He pushed off the back of the truck.

The EMT stepped in front of Reed. "Sir, that's not a good idea."

"Why not? Is she hurt badly?" The young guy was big, worked out, but Reed had no doubts he could take the guy down if necessary. Reed's hands fisted. His jaw muscle twitched.

"The others are working on her. I'm talking about you. I'd like to finish my exam, if that's okay."

The guy seemed to know Reed could take him down in a heartbeat. He reminded himself to stay cool. The EMT was only doing his job. No point in making it any harder for him.

Reed fished his wallet out of his pocket and produced his identification. "Name's Reed Campbell. I'm a Border Patrol agent. I have two brothers and two sisters. It's Monday at..." He checked his watch. "Four o'clock."

"Good. I think it's safe to say you didn't suffer a concussion. Will you let me patch up your forehead before you go, and let me take a look at what's causing all that blood on your shirt?" the young guy asked, resigned.

"Can't hurt." He sat still long enough for his gashes to be cleaned and bandaged.

"I still think it's a good idea for you to go to the hospital."

"I plan to." His gaze fixed on the team working on Emily.

"As a patient."

"I promise to get checked out if I take a turn for the worse."

"No changing your mind?"

"I appreciate all you're doing for me, but I'm more worried about her."

Reluctantly, the EMT produced papers. "Then I need your autograph on these. They say you received basic treatment at the scene and refused to be taken in for further medical evaluation."

Reed took them and signed off, uneasy that Emily was

still surrounded by a busy team of workers. If someone on the inside of his agency was helping Dueño, Reed couldn't chance his phone being hacked. His best bet was to play it cool with the EMT and pretend his had taken a hit. "Any chance I can borrow your phone? Mine's a casualty of the wreck, and I need to check in with my boss."

The worker nodded, handing over his cell.

They needed transportation, and Reed trusted a handful of people right now—most of whom shared his last name. His brothers were in North Texas, too far to catch a ride. His boss was his best bet. After being shot in the line of duty, Reed knew he could trust Gil. And with any luck, no one would be listening in on his boss's phone, either. Reed would play it cool just in case.

Gil picked up on the second ring.

"It's Reed. I had to borrow a phone. I don't have time to explain, but I need a car." There'd be a mountain of paperwork to deal with when this was settled.

"Where are you?"

"My Jeep's been totaled. I was chased off the road. This is big, Gil. Fingers are reaching out from over the border." Reed kept the name to himself to be on the safe side.

Gil muttered a curse.

"We need to be careful here," Reed warned. "We might have another Cal situation on our hands."

Gil grunted. "I'll have transportation waiting for you... Wait, let me think."

"How about the little place you like to visit on special Thursdays?" The Pelican restaurant in Galveston was Gil's wife's favorite seafood spot. He took her there every anniversary and occasionally on Thursday nights for their catfish special. Gil didn't go out on Fridays. Said it was too crowded. Few people knew Gil's habits the way Reed did. He'd learned a lot about his boss during the man's visits to the hospital after Reed was shot.

"Got it."

"Leave the keys so I can find them. The usual spot."

"Okay."

Keys would be under the sink in the bathroom. Reed glanced at Emily. The EMTs were still surrounding her. They'd want to take her to the hospital. With the amount of smoke she'd inhaled and the possible swelling, it was probably a good idea. "Can you get ahold of the local police chief? I'd like a fresh set of eyes on us at the hospital."

"I'll make the call myself from Vickie's personal cell."

His admin's number should be safe. "Appreciate it."

"You need a place to stay in the meantime?"

"I'll figure it out. Besides, the less I involve the department, the better. Probably best if I branch out on my own for this one." And he had no intention of leaving Emily for a second. These guys were relentless and she was scared. Not a good combination. If she made one mistake it'd be game over. The thought sent a lead fireball swirling down Reed's chest. Didn't need to get inside his head about why his reaction to the thought of anything happening to her was so strong. Reed passed it off as needing to keep his promises.

Gil paused. "Be careful."

"You know it." Reed ended the call. Now all he had to figure out was how to get to the bank and withdraw enough money to get by for a while. Then he'd need transportation from the hospital to The Pelican. No way could Emily walk in her current condition. She'd need time to rest and heal.

They didn't have the luxury of either.

Whoever was after her meant business.

The EMTs loaded her into the ambulance. Reed pushed through and took the step in an easy stride.

He was instantly pulled back.

"Sorry. It's policy. No one rides in back except us," one of the men said. He was older than the guy who'd worked on Reed.

"No exceptions?"

"Afraid not. How about you take a seat up front? We've already called a tow truck for your vehicle."

Reed nodded, not really liking the thought of being separated from Emily. Anything could happen to her in the back if those men were waiting, or worse yet, ambushed the ambulance.

Climbing into the cab, he told himself he cared only for professional reasons. The chance to nab a jerk who would do this to a woman fueled his need to protect her. And that it had nothing at all to do with the fact those hazel eyes of hers would haunt him in his sleep if he walked away.

Now that he knew her story had merit, he wanted to know more about her. It had everything to do with arming himself with knowledge that might just save both of their lives and nothing to do with the place in his heart she stirred, he lied.

Chapter Five

The long stretch of country road ahead provided too many opportunities for ambush. Reed reloaded his weapon, his gaze vacillating between looking ahead, to the sides and behind. "How much longer?"

"Fifteen minutes at the most."

"And the woman in back? How's she doing?" Reed glanced out the side-view mirror.

"My guys don't look as busy as they did on-site. That's a good sign in our line of work." He paused a beat. "They've been treating her for smoke inhalation. All I can tell you so far is that they're giving her oxygen, and she can expect to have a sore throat for a few days. Depending on the swelling in her throat, she might need to be intubated."

Reed didn't realize he'd cursed out loud until he saw the surprised look on the driver's face.

"She must be important to your case to get a reaction like that."

"I don't have one without her." Reed didn't appreciate women being beaten up, and especially not by men. His sister Lucy had received injuries as a teenager from an obsessed boyfriend. Reed chalked his current defensive feelings toward Emily up to bad memories.

"I notified my boss of the situation. He's calling ahead so the hospital will be ready with security."

"Thank you."

"She has a lot of other injuries and those might be of concern. Says she sustained them before the crash?"

Reed nodded.

"She needs a chest X-ray to ensure nothing's broken."

The way she'd been hugging her arms across her chest earlier now made more sense. He hadn't considered the possibility of cracked ribs. Anger bubbled to the surface. Reed muttered a string of curse words.

The EMT paused before continuing. "From the looks of it, she's been through hell and back. Those injuries could be far worse than the ones she sustained in the crash, but my guess is the doctor in charge is going to want to keep her for a while based on her pulse oximetry numbers."

"What's that?"

"Shows the amount of oxygen in the blood. Normal is one hundred and hers are ninety. She's experiencing some difficulty breathing, which leads me to believe her respiratory tract has some swelling."

"But she'll be okay?" In a matter of a few days she'd been beaten, starved and denied water. Reed's training and experience had taught him not to assume an injured person was telling the truth. In fact, most of the time they weren't. It was logic backed by years of experience. So why did he feel so damn awful about his earlier suspicions about her now? Was it the vulnerability in her eyes that hit him faster than a bullet and cut a similar hole in his chest? This case was different. Hell's bells, that statement didn't begin to scratch the surface.

"How long was she trapped in the Jeep?"

"Not more than eight or nine minutes."

"Less than ten minutes is good. That and the Jeep being open is a big help. With her oxygen levels being on the low side, best-case scenario is the damage to her airway and lungs is minimal. If there's no real swelling, she can expect a full recovery. We're almost there, by the way. The hospital is only a few minutes out. The doctor can tell you more after his exam. Her vital signs looked good."

"May I borrow your phone? I need to call work, and my cell didn't make it out of the Jeep," he lied. It was easier than explaining the whole situation.

The EMT glanced down at his cell, which was on the seat between them. "Be my guest."

Reed hoped his brother Luke would pick up.

"Hello?" The word was more accusation than greeting. Being in law enforcement made them suspicious of everything unfamiliar, and Luke wouldn't have recognized this number.

"It's Reed."

"What's up, baby bro?" Luke's stiff voice relaxed. "Leave your phone at a girl's house again?"

Reed ignored the joke. "I need help. I'm headed to ClearPond Regional Medical Hospital southeast of Houston with a hot package. I got a lot of eyes on me and fingers reaching from across the border."

"On my way." Bustling sounds of movement came through the line.

"Thanks." Reed would breathe a little easier when he had backup he could trust.

"I need to get anyone else involved?" Luke asked.

"Nah. I'm good with just you."

"Be there as fast as I can." More shuffling noises indicated Luke was already heading to his truck. "How can I reach you when I get close? I'm guessing your phone is toast."

"Yeah, that reminds me. Can you bring me Mom's old phone?" The saying was code for a burn phone, which couldn't be traced.

"Sure. Anything else?"

"Let Nick know what's going on."

"He's going to want to come." The Campbell boys had learned early in life to count on each other after their father had ditched the family and left their mother to bring up five kids on her own. Nick, the oldest, had taken over as a father figure.

"Tell him to stay put for now. I'll call when I need him."

"He may not listen."

"I can use any information he can dig up about a man they call Dueño. He's most likely running guns, trafficking women, but see if he can find anything else we can use to get to know this guy better."

"That should keep our brother busy. He still might want to come." Sounds of the truck door closing came through the line.

"Understood. I'll figure out what to do if he shows up. For now, try to discourage him." Reed totally understood his brother's need to be there. Reed would do the same thing if he were in Nick's shoes. "Let him know I can use him more on the sidelines right now. Plus, I'll have you to watch my back."

"Will do, baby bro."

Reed ended the call, thanked the driver and set his phone on the seat between them.

As promised, Reed saw the large white building ahead.

He surveyed the parking lot as they pulled inside the Emergency bay.

A Hispanic male stood by the corner of the building, smoking. He wore jeans, boots and a cowboy hat. The loose shirt he wore could easily hide a weapon. His head was tipped down, so Reed couldn't get a clear visual of the man's face.

The hospital was regional, so it was decent in size. There were a few dozen cars scattered around the parking lot, the heaviest concentration located closest to the main hospital entrance.

For a few seconds, Emily would be completely exposed while being wheeled inside. She'd be easy pickings for a trained sniper. Heck, any experienced gunman would be able to take her out faster than Reed could blink.

Luckily, there were no tall buildings nearby to gain a tactical advantage. A local hamburger joint, a taco-based fast-food chain restaurant and a gas station were located across the street. Those buildings weren't tall enough to matter.

Only an idiot would blitz them with a head-on attack. If this guy was smart and powerful enough to have a US presence, he didn't employ stupid people.

Reed's main concern was a bullet fired from in between the cars in the lot.

The gurney rolled through the sliding glass doors, where they were met by an officer. A sigh of relief passed Reed's lips once Emily was safely inside the building, but he wasn't ready to let his guard down.

The gurney was wheeled past an officer, and then disappeared inside a room. Reed paused at the door. "Your help is appreciated."

"I'll keep an officer here at all times and another at the elevator. The stairs are located at the end of the hall, so he'll be able to watch both exits from his vantage point." Reed had already counted the possible entry points and memorized the layout. Having someone centrally located was a good idea. Didn't hurt to have another officer right outside the door, as well.

"Hopefully, whoever is doing this will have enough sense to leave her alone for now. If not, your men should be a good deterrent." Reed couldn't be certain the officers appointed to watch over her could be trusted, but he was short on options.

Even if this one was honest, there was no way to know if the others were.

Cal had seemed honest and as if he was with the department for the right reasons. First impressions could be deceiving. Not only had Reed been ambushed and shot, his fiancée had been sleeping with Cal. The double deception had left him leery of trusting anyone whose last name wasn't Campbell.

Reed had doubted Gil for a while, too. But, his boss's true colors had come through when he'd maintained a bedside vigil next to Reed until he was out of the woods. Neither had stopped searching for Cal.

Letting Reed's guard down wasn't an option. He'd stay alert in Emily's room. He could rest when Luke arrived.

And Reed hoped like hell there wouldn't be any more surprises between now and then.

Stepping inside the bleached-white hospital room caused phantom pain to pierce his left shoulder—the exact spot where he'd taken a bullet. His attempt to take a step forward shut down midstride. *Shake it off.*

Forcing his boot to meet the white tile floor, he

couldn't suppress the shudder that ran through him after he pulled back the curtain and got a good look at Emily. Tubes stuck out of her from seemingly every direction. Monitors beeped.

With an uncomfortable smile on his lips, he moved closer.

As soon as she made eye contact, her face lit up. The tension in Reed's neck dissolved and warmth filled him. What was he supposed to do with that?

She lifted the oxygen mask off her face and quickly reined in her excitement, compressing her lips together instead. She could've been a poker player for the facade she put up now. Her even gaze dropped to the blanket covering her. "Thought maybe I'd scared you off."

"It takes more than a woman in trouble to make me run," he shot back, trying to get another smile from her. She didn't need to see the worry lines on his face. It would only make her panic.

A nurse fussed at Emily for lifting her mask. "I'll help you change into a gown." She turned to Reed. "You, sit. Or you'll have to go even though my boss gave me the rundown of the situation and you are law enforcement."

"Yes, ma'am." He took the chair closest to the bed, ignoring the uncomfortable feeling in his chest at seeing Emily look vulnerable and detached again. For her to have escaped the kind of man who could reach her from across a border, she had to be one tough cookie. Reed admired her for it. Hell, respected her even. Under different circumstances, she was the kind of woman he could see himself spending time getting to know better. Experience had taught him to keep his business and private lives separate.

Reed had no plans to break his rule no matter how

much the scared little thing in the bed next to him tugged at his heart strings. *Scared? Little?* He almost cracked a smile. From what he could tell so far, she wouldn't like being referred to as either.

Compared with his six-foot-two frame, most people would be considered small. Besides, it was normal to feel something for a woman in her circumstances. He wouldn't be human if his protective instincts didn't flare every time he saw the bruising on what would otherwise be considered silky, delicate skin. A woman like her should be cherished, not beaten.

The thought of the men in the parking lot waiting to make sure those hazel eyes closed permanently sobered Reed's thoughts. "How are you really feeling?"

A small woman in a white coat pushed past the nurse and introduced herself to Emily before she answered.

Reed sat patiently by as the doctor performed her exam. Based on how much attention Emily had received on the scene and when she'd first arrived at the hospital, he figured they wouldn't be letting her go tonight.

Reed had mixed feelings about her release. He couldn't be certain they were secure here at the facility—hell, in this town. And yet, she'd been in pretty bad shape when he found her. He couldn't deny her the medical attention she needed. The crash had made her physical condition even worse. Even if he had wanted to run her in for questioning, he doubted she would've made it through the interrogation without collapsing from exhaustion.

Then again, he knew better than to underestimate the power of fear. And *scared* didn't begin to describe the woman he'd found on the docks.

The doctor scribbled notes on the chart as she examined Emily.

He recognized the bag of saline. Good. She needed hydration, and that would be the quickest way. She'd already gone through a bag during the ambulance ride, according to the EMT. Her skin already looked pinker, livelier.

A nurse gently washed Emily's face and then blotted ointment. "Your sunburn is healing. This'll speed up the process."

Keeping her alive wasn't the only problem Reed had. He needed to see if Dueño's men had broken into Emily's town house and found the passwords.

The doctor abruptly turned on Reed. "I understand you were driving the vehicle before it crashed?"

Reed introduced himself, producing his badge. "That's correct, ma'am. How is she?"

"So far, so good. We won't know the extent of the swelling for another couple of hours." The doctor gently pinched the skin on Emily's forearm. "She's severely dehydrated."

"She went without water for several days."

A look of sympathy crossed the doctor's features. "Then we'll want to keep her on the IVs, slowly introduce her to solid food." She turned to the nurse. "Start with a clear liquid diet, advance to full liquids, soft and then regular."

"She managed to eat half a hamburger earlier."

"That's encouraging."

"How soon will she recover?"

"Good question. A lot depends on her. But because of the smoke inhalation, I'm apprehensive. She's been having some difficulty breathing due to a swollen respiratory tract. Since she's getting to the ER so late, I'll want to keep her overnight at a minimum to ensure the swelling subsides. We need to keep a read on her arterial blood gases, too."

Reed's lips compressed in a frown. He leaned closer to the doctor when he said, "Doesn't sound good."

"My inspection of her airway is encouraging. Edema is minimal—"

Reed must've given her a look without realizing it because the doctor stopped midsentence.

"The swelling isn't bad. Of course, with any smoke inhalation I'm concerned about the swelling increasing in twenty-four to forty-eight hours. I'm holding off on intubation for now. I'll be keeping a close eye on her, though. Any movement there and I'll have no choice. I've already given her a dose of steroids, and the nurse will give her a bronchodilator treatment."

The thought she needed help to keep her throat from swelling shut didn't encourage Reed. "What about her other injuries?"

"We won't know until we dig a little deeper. I'll send in a tech to take her for X-rays after her breathing treatment."

"I'm responsible for her safety. Any chance I can tag along?"

"Shouldn't be a problem. I'll make a note on her file." The doctor's gaze intensified on Reed. "How about you? Mind if I take a look while you're here?"

"Me? Nah. I'm fine."

"Looks like your forehead took impact and you have substantial bleeding on your shirt. I'd feel a lot better if you'd let me take a look."

"It's just a scratch."

The doctor held her ground. "Even so, I'd like to examine you while the nurse administers treatment."

Reed focused on Emily, who was being told to inhale medicine from a tube.

The doctor kept her gaze on him. "My brother-in-law is a firefighter. His job is to help everyone else, but he's the last person to ask when he needs it."

"A job hazard," Reed joked, trying to redirect the seriousness of the conversation. "If it'll make you feel better, go ahead."

The doctor examined him, cleaned his cuts and brought in another nurse, instructing her to bandage his wounds.

"I'll check in on you both later," she said before making a move toward the door.

"Can those treatments stop the swelling?" Reed inclined his head toward Emily.

"That's the hope," the doctor said. "Like I said, we'll have to keep her overnight for observation to be sure."

Reed hoped they had that long. He didn't like feeling this exposed, and he couldn't be sure he could trust local police. Aches and pains from the day hit hard and fast. His brother would arrive in a few hours and then Reed could get some rest.

Until then, he didn't plan to take his eyes off Emily.

WHATEVER THE DOCTOR had ordered was working wonders on Emily. Her head had stopped pounding, and her body didn't feel as if she'd been run through a cheese grater any longer. News about the results from the X-rays had been promised.

A glance at the clock said she'd been in the hospital for two hours already. Had she dozed off?

She didn't dare move for fear she'd wake the agent slumped in the chair next to her bed. He needed rest.

Other than a bandage on his forehead and chest, he'd refused medical treatment. He'd taken the nurse up on her offer of soap, a washcloth and dental supplies. He'd washed in the bathroom and stripped down to a basic white T-shirt he'd borrowed from one of the orderlies before leaning back in the lounge chair and closing his eyes. His T was the only thing basic about him. His job would require a toned body. One glance at the muscled agent said he took his profession seriously.

His rock-hard abs moved up and down with every even breath he took. The rest of him was just as solid and in control.

Emily reached for the water he'd placed near her head on the cart next to her.

"How was your nap?"

She suppressed a yelp. "You startled me."

"Sorry."

"I thought you were out." She took a sip.

"I'm a light sleeper."

Of course he was. A man who was always prepared for the worst-case scenario wouldn't zone out completely. "How long have you been in your job?"

"Six years."

Emily had been in her job half that time. She worried the only steady thing in her life would be gone by the time she returned to Plano.

But a man who looked like Reed Campbell must have a wife waiting for him. "The hours have to be difficult on your family."

"You might be surprised. One of my brothers is a US marshal, the other is FBI." He cracked a smile, and her heart skipped a beat. "My sisters aren't much better. One's a police officer in Plano and the other's a victims' rights advocate for the sheriff. Guess you could say law enforcement runs in our blood."

"Wow. That's impressive. I was actually thinking about your wife and kids."

He shook his head. "No wife. No kids."

"A committed bachelor?"

"No time."

She almost believed him, until the corner of his full lip curled. Surely, a tough and strong man who looked like him attracted plenty of women. "Are you teasing?"

"It's been a tough day." He scrubbed a hand over the scruff on his face. Lightness left his expression. "How are you holding up, really?"

"They seem to be patching me up okay." Why couldn't she admit how much pain she was actually in or how scared she was about her future? A part of her wanted to believe the agent cared how she was actually doing, and not just making polite conversation, or ensuring his witness could testify. Besides, she couldn't remember the last time she'd opened up to someone. Heck, she'd made herself a loner at the House when she wasn't feeding or bathing one of her half siblings. She'd skillfully hidden behind attending to them. "I took a few bumps. I'll be good as new by morning."

He shot her a look. "Okay, tough guy. I'm not buying that."

Most likely, he needed to assess her condition to see if she was stable enough to travel or go on the run. Duh. What a dummy. She'd almost convinced herself the hunky agent actually cared about her. Wow, she must've taken more damage to the head than she realized. "He'll come for me here, won't he?"

He eyed her for a long moment without speaking. "Suspicious men are already stationed outside."

Was he trying to figure out if he could trust her? "I know my story sounds crazy."

"I've heard worse."

Of course he had in his line of work. "Maybe it just sounds bizarre in my head."

"It's normal to need a minute to let this sink in. Your world was just turned on its head. It'll take a bit to absorb. Don't be hard on yourself. I've seen grown men buckle under lesser circumstances."

Was that a hint of pride in his brilliant brown eyes? Or was she seeing something she wanted to see instead of reality? This was most likely the speech he gave to all the victims he came across. *Victim?* The word sat bitterly on her tongue. She may have had a rough childhood and she might be in sticky circumstances now, but no way was she a helpless victim. "This might sound weird. I mean, we've only just met. But, I feel like I *know* you."

"We've been through hell and back. It forms a bond." A wide smile broke across white teeth, shattering his serious persona.

Emily forced her gaze from his lips.

Chapter Six

Experience had taught Emily the best way to dispel the mystery of someone was the reality of getting to know them. And the last thing she needed was for the agent to realize she was attracted to him. Heck, she'd wanted to crawl under the bed and hide earlier when he walked in the room and she grinned like an idiot. Hopefully, she'd reined it in before she'd made a complete fool out of herself. "You said earlier that you came from a big family?"

"You'll meet one of my brothers in an hour. Luke's the one who works for the FBI." Reed popped to his feet and walked to the window, his thigh muscles pressing against his jeans as they stretched. He had the power and athletic grace of a predator closing in on its meal. His gaze narrowed as he peered out the window.

"Maybe the doctor will let me go tomorrow." She glanced at the door and back to Reed. "It doesn't seem safe for us here."

"All I need for you to do is rest and get as strong as you can." He didn't say because they might need to bolt at any moment, although the tension radiating from his body told her exactly what he was thinking.

"What about you? You ever sleep?"

"Not much when I'm working on a case. Speaking of

which, we should talk about yours." He moved back to his seat, but positioned himself on the edge and rested his elbows on his knees.

"You already know I work at a computer company. That pretty much sums up my life. I'm in line for a promotion, so I've been working nonstop for months. It's part of why I panicked when you called my boss." Telling the handsome agent work was all she had, made her life sound incredibly small and empty. Speaking of which, what would Jared think when she showed up to work Monday looking as if she'd been the warm-up punching bag for an MMA fighter? Her boss was a climber, and she knew he used her to do much of his own work under the guise of training her. Was there any way to finagle more time off without jeopardizing her position?

A lump of dread sat in her stomach. How could she go back at all now? With a man like Dueño chasing her, would she even be able to pick up her old life where she'd left off? She focused on the agent. "How do we keep me alive?"

"I could talk to my brother Nick about witness protection. He's a US marshal."

And leave behind everything she'd worked for? It was sad that her first thought was dreading having to start all over with a new job, and not that she'd be leaving her friends and family behind. A bitter stab of loneliness pierced the center of Emily's chest.

Her reaction must've been written all over her face because Reed was on his feet, his gaze locked on hers. "It's just an option. I'm not saying we have to go through with it. I wouldn't be able to leave my family behind, either."

At least he couldn't read her mind. A man like him with more family around than he could count wouldn't understand her desperation at leaving behind the only thing she'd ever been able to count on. Work. The sadness in that thought weighted her limbs. Emily refused to give in, crossing her arms.

"It's okay. It's a reasonable option. I should definitely give it some serious consideration." She hoped the agent didn't pick up on the fact there was no emotion in those last words.

"I just thought we should explore every possibility of keeping you safe until we can put this jerk behind bars." Whereas her words might've lacked emotion, the venom in his when he said the word *jerk* was its own presence in the room.

Emily had always believed that she was making the best out of the situation she'd been handed. Being successful at work was so much less complicated than dealing with people and especially family. She'd never minded being alone before. In fact, she'd preferred it. So why did it suddenly feel like a death sentence?

Wasn't getting the chance for a new identity, a fresh start in life, the ideal solution to many of her problems? As much as she didn't want to leave the life she'd built in Plano, the option had to be considered. "How does witness protection work exactly?"

"We could talk to my brother to get all the facts, but you'd be assigned to a US marshal who'd become responsible for giving you a new identity, a place to live and a job somewhere no one would know to look for you."

"And contact with my family?"

His gaze dropped to the floor. "I'm afraid that's not possible."

Even though she spoke to her mother only a few times a year, Emily couldn't imagine cutting off that last little connection to her past, to her. "And what if that's not possible?"

"Do you remember anything about the person who did this to you?"

"No. I didn't see him at all. They were careful about protecting him. All I heard was his voice. I'd know that sound if I heard it again." She paused a beat. "Which isn't much to go on, is it?"

"It's something," he said encouragingly.

"Not enough for an arrest, though, let alone a conviction."

He didn't make eye contact when he said, "No. But maybe you can lead us to his hideout. We've already been able to pinpoint the area of abduction, and these guys tend to be territorial."

She told him the name of the resort where she'd stayed, and everything else she could remember about her abduction, which was precious little since she'd been blindfolded most of the time. "That's where it gets even worse. I mean, I wish I could give you more to work with. I was blindfolded for much of the walk, which felt like it took forever."

"These guys are professionals. It's not your fault. We have the location of your abduction. They didn't take you anywhere by plane, right?"

"No. We walked the entire time."

"That gives us a starting point."

"Except that we could've been walking in circles for all I knew."

"Believe it or not, you've narrowed down the possibilities with what you've told me so far. It's a start." Reed stabbed his fingers through his thick dark hair. "Anyone have a spare key to your town house?"

Like a friend? Emily almost choked on her own laughter—laughter that she held deep inside because if it came out, so would the onslaught of tears. "No."

His dark brow arched. "Not even a neighbor or your landlord?"

"I own it." Emily didn't address the bit about the neighbor. She didn't want to admit she didn't know the people who lived around her. A casualty of working too many long nights and weekends, she decided. Her life had never seemed empty to her before, so why did it now? Without her job, her career, it would be.

She'd worked too hard to let it all be taken away by some crazed criminal. What if she told her boss about the car crash? Maybe she could convince Jared to give her an extended leave of absence and save her job. It wasn't as if she took days off. With her rollover vacation days, she could take off two months. That might give the agent a chance to catch Dueño, and she could restore her life. She might have invested a lot of time in her work, but it was all she had. And if Jared asked too many questions or figured out her half-truth, she might not have that anymore. Maybe she could tell him what had happened. On second thought, there was no gray area with Jared. How many times had he fired someone for a slight infraction? Even though she hadn't broken any company rules, he would assume she'd done something to bring this on herself. He'd start viewing her as a threat to the company and find a reason to get rid of her.

The thought of giving up everything she'd worked for sucked all the air out of her lungs. Hadn't she fought long and hard to put down roots? Her place in Texas was home. "It seems like witness protection is my only option, but what if I don't want it?"

Reed ran a hand over the scruff on his chin. "We catch this guy and you're home free. Otherwise, we wait it out and keep you safe. My experience with men like these is that they have a short memory. If I can get you safely through a few weeks, you should be in the clear."

Was returning to her life in a few weeks really an option? Surely, she could get that much time off. The first real spark of hope in days lit inside her. Maybe she wouldn't have to give up the only life that felt like hers. "What if these people are different and don't mind waiting it out? How will we know for sure?"

The intensity in his brown eyes increased. "My brother Nick is digging deeper to find out their story. He'll be able to tell us what we're facing. My plan is to catch them and put them in jail where they belong."

"I could make up a story for my boss. Take time off."

Reed gave her a look as if he understood. Did he? No way could he get that she wasn't staying because of family or friends. He probably had more of those than he could count, too. How did she tell someone who had so many relationships worth living for the real reason she wanted to keep her life was because of her work? Or maybe she needed to dig in and fight for the small life she had. There wasn't much else she could be sure of right now except that she couldn't bear the thought of losing everything again as she had when she was a little girl and the only life she'd ever known had been stripped away from her. "Things get too intense, can I change my mind?"

"WitSec will always be an option."

"And what about you? What will happen to you if I go in?" She hadn't considered the agent before. Wouldn't her going into the program take him out of the line of fire? "I don't want to put you in any more danger."

"This is my job. Besides, I want to catch this son of a bitch as much as you."

WHETHER EMILY WENT into WitSec or not, Reed had every intention of seeing this case through to the end. A bad agent had infected the agency. Reed needed to find out who before someone else got shot, or worse, killed.

At least Emily's story had checked out with her boss. Reed had almost asked his brother to investigate her background. He was still scratching his head as to why he hadn't. The only people he didn't run background checks on were the women he dated, which put him in unfamiliar territory with his witness. He'd have to gain her trust and actually have a conversation with her to find out what he wanted to know. And then, he'd have to trust she'd told the truth.

Trust? Interesting word. Other than his boss, Reed hadn't trusted anyone who didn't share his last name in the past year. He was bad at it. And yet, gaining hers might be the key to unlocking who in his agency was involved in this. He'd always suspected Cal wasn't the only bad crop in the garden.

Reed could give up a little about himself if it meant advancing his case. There were other reasons compelling him to open up a little to this witness, too. None of which he wanted to explore. The image of her smile—the one like when he'd first walked in—stamped his thoughts. She'd suppressed it faster than a squirrel hides its supper, but for the second it was there, her whole face shone. "Someone in my agency is corrupt. I have every intention of finding out who they are and bringing them to justice."

Her gaze intensified. "That part of your code of honor?"

"It's more than that." Uneasy and unsure if he was about to do the right thing, he pulled up his T-shirt and turned to let her see the scar on his left shoulder.

"Ohmygosh. What happened to you?" The warmth in her voice would melt an iceberg.

It drew him in and made him want to connect with it. He lowered the hem of his shirt and returned to his spot on the edge of the chair, making sure he maintained visual contact with the door in his peripheral. The thought of discussing what had happened to him a year ago parked an RV on his chest.

He took a breath and shoved past the feeling. "While on a case a year ago, I got a hot tip on a kidnapping ring. Young girls were being snatched, shuffled across the border and sold before their parents even knew they were missing. Heard a few were holed up and drugged in a house near the border. I'd been tracking a coyote for two years." He paused when her eyebrow shot up. "Human trafficker. Seemed like he knew every time I got close. He'd up and relocate his business. Goes without saying how badly I wanted to put this guy away and toss the key for what he was doing to those young girls. And yet, I was careful not to make a mistake. I was so close I could almost taste it."

"So what happened?"

"This guy had big connections on both sides of the border. He was under the protection of a rebel leader. And that guy had a border patrol agent on his payroll. He discovered I was about to bust the coyote, so… Let's just say I was set up. Wasn't supposed to walk out of the hot spot they'd sent me to. Thought I was close to this guy. Turns out, he was closer to my fiancée."

"Oh." The flash in her eyes went from sympathy to indignant. "Two people you trusted betrayed you? That must make it hard to believe in anyone else."

She had no idea. Or, did she?

There was a subtle lilt to her tone, an unspoken kinship that said she might know exactly what he was talking about. Had someone she'd trusted turned on her? "I spent a little time in a room just like this one. Gave me a lot of time to think. Figure a man should be left alone with his thoughts for about two minutes before he turns against the world."

She didn't laugh at his joke meant to lighten the mood.

"What happened to the people who did that to you?" There was an all-too-familiar anger in her voice now.

"He disappeared across the border before he could be arrested. Someone has him tucked away nicely because not one of our informants has seen him."

"And the woman?"

"Could be with him for all we know." He paused. "She didn't exactly break the law."

"I'm so sorry. Having people you trust turn on you is one thing, but then never having him brought to justice adds a whole new level of unfairness."

The depths of her eyes said she knew about unfair. What had happened in her life for her to be able to sympathize? More questions he didn't have answers to.

A knock at the door brought Reed to his feet, his weapon drawn and leading the way as he stalked toward the entrance to the room.

"There's someone here to see you, Agent Campbell." Reed recognized the voice as belonging to the officer. "His ID says he's Special Agent Luke Campbell."

The past few hours had soared by. What was it about

talking to Emily that made time disappear and the ache in his chest lighter?

"My brother's here," Luke said to ease the tension he felt coming from Emily. Her compassion had melted a little of the ice encasing his heart. Relieved for the break, Reed wasn't ready to let anyone inside. And yet, talking to her had come easier than he'd expected. Even more surprising was the fact that he wanted to tell her more.

"Send him in." Reed kept his weapon drawn on the off chance someone other than his brother walked through that door, refusing to be caught off guard again. It was unlikely anyone would know he'd called his brother, but taking chances was for gamblers—and Reed didn't bet on odds.

"It's me." His brother seemed to understand Reed's apprehension as he walked through the door with his hands up in the universal sign for surrender.

Reed lowered his weapon and returned it to his holster. He greeted his brother with a bear hug and introduced him to Emily, surprised to see a tear roll down her cheek.

"Nice to meet you," she said quickly. Her unreadable expression returned so fast Reed almost thought he'd imagined her brief show of emotion.

Reed caught a glimpse of his brother's reaction to seeing the bruising on her face as Luke handed over the burn phone he'd brought. No Campbell man would take lightly to a woman being beaten, even though they saw it far too often in their lines of work.

"We have a lot of company outside." Luke leaned against the wall near the big window facing the door, and crossed his ankles. Another habit formed on the job— they never put their backs to the door.

"I saw a couple when we came in."

"There's half a dozen now, covering all entrances. One looked twice at me even though I kept my head down." He wore a ball cap, T-shirt and jeans. "I'm guessing they saw the resemblance."

"You two do look a lot alike," Emily agreed.

Reed couldn't argue. So, the men might just think it was Luke leaving when Reed ducked out later. Now that Luke was there, Reed could risk leaving Emily's side without fearing for her safety. "I have to run out in a bit. Mind if we switch hats?"

Luke shook his head and pulled off his ball cap. "Make sure you pull it down low, over your bandage. Looks like you took a pretty good hit."

"I'm fine."

Emily coughed loudly enough to let everyone know she'd done it on purpose. "Um, he pulled me out of a burning car while fighting off men shooting at us. He has to be exhausted. I don't think he should be going anywhere."

Reed had to fist his hands to stop from wiping the smile off his brother's face.

"What did I say?" Emily's gaze bounced from one to the other.

They stood, staring, daring the other to speak first.

"Nothing," Reed said too quickly. He didn't want to share the fact that both of his brothers had fallen in love with women they were protecting. "My brother just has a twisted sense of humor."

Luke turned to her. "I want the same thing you do for my brother."

"Rest?" she asked, puzzled.

"Peace."

When no one explained what Luke meant, Emily shrugged.

Reed handed over his Stetson.

"I think I'm getting the better deal out of this exchange," Luke joked, replacing his ball cap with the white cowboy hat.

"We'd better trade shirts, too," Reed said.

"Can I see you for a second, Reed?" Emily asked. "Privately?"

Luke's gaze locked onto Reed's. He nodded.

His brother excused himself to the bathroom.

"Everything okay?" The fear Emily's condition was getting worse gripped Reed faster than if he'd walked into an intersection and had been hit by a bus.

"Come closer?"

Reed moved to the side of her bed.

She patted the sheets, and he took her cue to sit down next to her. The nurse had helped her shower, and Emily looked even more beautiful. This close, she smelled clean and flowery.

"I'm scared." The words came out in a whisper.

Those fearful hazel eyes were back, the ones threatening to crack more of the ice encasing his heart, and his pulse raced.

For lack of a better way to offer reassurance, he bent down and gently kissed her forehead. "My brother's the best. You'll be safe."

She shook her head, her gaze locked onto his the whole time. "I know. I'm afraid for you."

The warmth of a thousand campfires flooded his chest. Hell's bells. What was he supposed to do with that?

He opened his mouth to speak, but her hands were

already tunneled into his hair, urging him closer. Last thing he wanted to do was hurt her, so he stopped the second their lips touched, waiting for a sign from her she was still okay.

Her tongue darted inside his mouth, and he had to remind himself not to take control. She knew what she could handle, what hurt, so he momentarily surrendered to her judgment, careful not to apply any more pressure than she could handle.

Those soft pink lips of hers nearly did him in. Every muscle in his body was strung so tight he thought they might snap. He wanted more.

For her, he would hold back.

As her tongue searched inside his mouth, he brought his hands up to cup her face.

A noise from the bathroom caused Reed to pull back first.

Emily brought her hand up to her lips, her nervous "tell." "I'm sorry. I probably shouldn't have done that."

"It's a good thing you did."

She smiled and those thousand campfires burst into flames.

"I know you're going to search down the agent who called before everything went crazy."

He didn't deny it.

"Just be careful. And come back." The sincerity in her eyes nearly knocked him back. Her concern was outlined in the wrinkles in her forehead.

He bent down and kissed them. Then he feathered kisses on the tip of her nose, her eyelids.

Not a lot made sense to him right now except this moment happening between them. Underneath the bruises and the bad bleach job, there was a beautiful woman.

And he was a man.

Their lives had been in danger and they'd both nearly been killed today.

Reed couldn't be sure if this was the beginning of real sparks between the two of them or if the attraction was down to basic primal urges and they both needed proof of life, but for a split second, his defenses lowered and she inched inside his heart.

Chapter Seven

The faucet turned on in the bathroom, and Reed heard the rush of water in the sink. He figured it was Luke's polite way of saying he was done hiding.

Reed needed to get moving, anyway. He stood. "All clear."

Emily blinked up at him. "Remember what I said."

"Try to get some rest." He grazed the soft skin of her arm with the tip of his finger. He needed to catch these guys and give Emily her life back.

She closed her eyes and smiled.

"Here's what you need to know before you head out." Luke quietly reentered the room. "Dueño is believed to be a ghost. No one's seen him. Some people aren't even sure if he exists, but if something's illegal and it touches South America, his name shows up every time."

Emily blinked her eyes open. "I've seen him. He's real."

"Our lowlife owns those distribution channels?" Reed asked.

"The guy can get any product moved for a price." Luke's gaze moved from Emily to Reed. "Makes a lot of money on women and children."

Reed muttered a curse. "What else?"

"Like I mentioned, he stays out of the spotlight. No one's seen him. He's like a damn phantom."

"So he likes to hide. Makes it easier to stay under the radar that way."

"And harder to convict," Luke agreed. "He has several high-ranking lieutenants. Marco Delgado, Julian Escado and Jesus Ramirez are at the top."

"I've heard of Ramirez, but not the others. His name was associated with Cal's, but I thought he worked alone."

"I remember. Dueño set up the teams in supercells, so they'd be harder to trace back to him. This group plays their cards close to their vest. Nick found out they have a meeting once a year at Dueño's compound to discuss business. Other than that, there's no communication."

"Makes it hard to track their activity back to him."

"And that's one of the biggest benefits. Has its risks, too."

Reed rocked his head. "Any one of them could go rogue and Dueño wouldn't know about it for a while."

"The lieutenants know each other, obviously, but the men in the ranks don't know they all work in the same organization. Word on the street is that these three are heads of their own groups. Members view each other as competition."

"A misunderstanding and they could end up killing one of their own without knowing it." Reed rubbed the scruff on his chin.

"True."

"If they think they're turning in a rival, we might get them to talk about each other." Reed pinched the bridge of his nose to stem the dull ache forming. This was bigger than he'd imagined. Emily was in grave danger. "Do the low-ranking guys know about the summit?"

"Some do. They think the guys are meeting next week to agree on territory."

"We might be able to get one of our informants to speak. Any idea where this compound is located?"

"Unfortunately, no. It's impossible to get anyone to talk. They're afraid of repercussion. The organization is well run."

"We might know a link. An agent phoned after I pulled away from the docks, asking if he could take her in for me." Reed stopped long enough to pace. "Besides, men who run things for others get greedy. They end up asking why they should do all the work for someone else's gain. Maybe we can figure out a way to pit them against each other."

"Your guy might be the connection we're looking for." Luke grabbed his keys and tossed them to Reed with a grin. "Bring it back in one piece. You know how I love that truck."

"We'll see." Reed glanced at Emily, again thankful her eyes were closed and her breath even. "Take care of her. She's been through a lot."

"You know I will, baby bro."

Reed hugged his brother, the manly kind of hug with backslaps.

Keeping his head low, he tucked his hands in his front jeans pockets and strolled down the hall. Dueño's men would have all the exits covered. The trick would be getting to Luke's truck without being noticed.

It was long past midnight. The darkness should help. Although, it also meant there'd be fewer people coming in and out of the hospital.

Reed took the stairs to the bottom floor and, by memory, located the ER. There was no one in the long hallway leading to the parking lot where he'd initially entered the building. An eerie quiet settled over him.

The click of his boots was the only sound as he entered the sterile white passage.

Going outside without a cover was a bad idea. Last thing he needed was someone following him. Maybe he could grab some coffee in the waiting room, bide his time until someone left.

An agonizing forty-three minutes later, he got his chance as a family left with their teenager. His arm was heavily bandaged, and his washed-out expression said he'd most likely been drinking and had done something stupid to get hurt. The young man had to be six foot and close to two hundred pounds. He took after his father. The pair should offer plenty of cover.

Reed shadowed the family, breaking off in the parking lot as he ducked in between two cars. He located his brother's truck, which was exactly where he'd said it would be. Reed kept his head down as he climbed in the cab. His thoughts focused on Agent Stephen Taylor—get to him and find the answers.

He located the family's car as they pulled out of the parking lot and followed.

A quick call to his boss on the burn phone Luke had provided and Reed had Gil updated and working on finding Agent Taylor's home address inside of ten minutes. Double that, and Luke was on the expressway, blending in to his surroundings. His tail had given up fifteen minutes ago, figuring, as Reed had hoped, that he was part of the family leaving and not a person of interest. It most likely hadn't hurt that Luke had come in twenty minutes before Reed left.

No matter how quickly he returned to the hospital,

his sense of unease about leaving would still produce a lump in his gut. Even though Luke was capable of handling any situation he encountered, he was one man and these guys had brought an army.

Emily's bruised face and vulnerable eyes pierced his thoughts.

His cell buzzed and he realized how tightly he'd been gripping the steering wheel. The text came. Stephen Taylor's address. Reed pulled off the highway and plugged in the location to Luke's GPS.

Another fifteen minutes and Reed was in the neighborhood.

Taylor's street was dark, save for a streetlight next to his house. Reed crept past the front of the one-story ranch house and then rounded the block. There could be a fortress inside and Taylor could be waiting. No doubt, he'd be on edge if he was close to Dueño.

Reed shut off his lights and parked down the street. He put on the Kevlar vest in the backseat of the cab, and then palmed his weapon.

With his Glock leveled and leading the way, he moved along the shrubbery, saying a little prayer no dogs would bark.

The home was a simple brick ranch. More details about Taylor came through via text. Turned out, Taylor had a wife and a baby. He was the last person Reed would suspect to be dirty but then again he had no idea what the guy's personal situation was, and greed was a powerful motivator. Cases like these had a color. Green.

None of this place fit. This was a nice middle-class neighborhood. Wouldn't a dirty agent live in a nicer house? There was nothing wrong with this one, but it was definitely something Taylor could afford on his own.

He didn't need a side income for this. If an agent was dirty, there were clues. They'd live in a house clearly above their pay grade or have expensive hobbies, such as collecting sports cars.

Maybe the guy was in debt. He could have a sick kid or a gambling problem. If he was really smart, he'd give the appearance of living off his means and sock the money away for the future. Men who planned for the long-term usually had more sense than to get involved with criminals.

Blackmail? There were other possibilities Reed considered as he surveyed the perimeter, allowing his eyes the chance to adjust to the dark. The curtains in the living room had been left open. The slats in the two-inch wood blinds provided enough of a gap to get a clear view into the living room. Nothing stood out. The furnishings were simple and had a woman's touch. A baby swing, playpen and toys crowded the place. Not one thing looked out of the ordinary for a young family of three.

Reed could plainly see through to the back door into the kitchen. No keypad for an alarm system. He changed his vantage point. No sign of one near the front door, either.

No alarm system. No dog. No real security.

He'd expected the guy to be paranoid.

Another piece of the puzzle that didn't fit.

Reed ran his hand along the windowsills, looking for a good place to enter the home. He didn't care how careful this guy was. Reed had every intention of getting answers tonight.

The windows and doors were all locked. Twelve windows and two doors were possible exit points. Reed peeked in each, memorizing the layout before returning to his spot. The front door was made of solid wood, which made it difficult to breach without making too much noise. Reed's best bet would be to enter through the kitchen. The top half of the door was glass. He shucked the vest, and took off his T-shirt and wrapped it around his hand like tape on a boxer's fist.

A dog barked. Reed bit out a curse and worked faster. No way was he leaving without questioning Taylor. This guy was the ticket to putting the puzzle pieces together. Memories of the night Reed was shot flooded him. Reed battled to force them away and stay focused.

He punched through the glass and then unlocked the door. A few seconds later, his T-shirt and Kevlar was on. He wasn't taking another chance with a dirty agent.

The house was quiet save for the ticking clock hanging on the wall in the kitchen. Reed cleared the room and rounded the corner toward the bedrooms, his weapon leading the way, and froze. From three feet away, the business end of a Glock was aimed at his face, most likely right between his eyes.

"What are you doing here, Agent Campbell?" Stephen asked.

"Put your gun down and I'll explain." Reed intentionally kept his voice calm and low.

"Not until you tell me what's going on." Stephen's hands shook and he didn't lower his weapon.

Reed leveled his, aiming for the chest. Stephen wore pajama pants and a T-shirt. He hadn't had time to put on his Kevlar. One shot and his chest would have a hole. Reed said a silent prayer he'd get his shot off first. Kevlar didn't help with a bullet in the head. Both were trained shooters, a requirement of the job. "We need to talk."

"In the middle of the night? What the hell could be this important?"

Neither made a move to put down his weapon.

"It's about the woman." Reed took a step back, inching toward the corner, anything that could be a barrier or slow down a bullet. If this guy was in league with a man like Dueño, he'd have no problem doing away with anyone or anything that got in his way. And yet, nothing about his house said he was on the take. There were signs with Cal. He'd driven a fifty-thousand-dollar car. Lived in a neighborhood a little too pricey for his pay grade. He'd chalked it all up to rich parents and a partial trust fund. If anyone had bothered to take a closer look or check his file, they'd have realized his parents were blue-collar workers from Brownsville. But then, it wasn't as if Cal had invited anyone from the department over to his place for backyard barbecues. And he'd been smart about it. He lived in a nice house but not so expensive it would draw attention.

None of those signs was present here at Stephen's. His place looked as if he lived on the paycheck provided by the agency. Then again, looks could be deceiving. He'd also believed his fiancée when she'd said there was nothing going on between Cal and her.

Stephen stepped forward. "What are you talking about?"

"You called me earlier this afternoon. Asked to run in my witness for me."

"Yeah. So what? Thought I was doing you a favor."

Right. Reed wasn't about to let Stephen off with that pat answer. "Since when would anyone want to take on filling out someone else's paperwork?"

Stephen didn't respond. Reed was pretty certain if he

could peel back the guy's skull Reed would see fireworks going off in there.

"You plan to shoot me?" he hedged.

"Not unless you fire first."

"Then why don't we both put our weapons down and talk?" In a show of good faith, Reed lowered his first. He was close enough to the corner to make a fast break if this didn't go as planned.

Stephen lowered his weapon at the same time a baby wailed in the next room. On edge, he bit out a curse and shot a stern look to Reed. "Wait here. And don't you move."

"I'm not going anywhere until I get answers." Reed tucked his gun in his holster, and then crossed his arms over his chest.

"Good." He moved to the end of the hall where the master bedroom was located. "Kiera, the baby's up. I'm in the kitchen with a work friend, and we need to finish our business."

Reed didn't hear her response, but she must've agreed because Stephen turned his attention back to Reed and urged him into the kitchen.

"What the hell's going on?" Stephen asked. Confusion mixed with the daggers being shot from his glare.

"You tell me."

"Tell you what?" he parroted.

"Why'd you feel the need to relieve me of my passenger?" Reed followed Stephen's gaze to the broken glass on the kitchen floor.

"Great." He moved to the pantry, retrieved a broom and started sweeping up the shards. "My baby plays on this floor. And, my wife is going to be pissed when she sees this. You know, you could've knocked."

Well, hell in a handbasket, Reed really was mixed up now. "Stop sweeping and fill me in."

"My wife'll be in to get a bottle, so I can't stop sweeping. She's going to be pissed enough as it is."

Nothing about Stephen's actions said he was anything but a family man. Reed sighed sharply. "If you didn't want my witness, why'd you call and ask for her?"

The sound of crying intensified. Stephen glanced toward the hall. "Grab a bottle from the fridge, and put it in the microwave for a minute and a half."

Reed did as he was told, sticking the glass bottle in the microwave.

"Take the lid off first. Don't you know anything about babies?" Stephen's pleading look would've been funny under different circumstances. Even a tough guy like him seemed to know better than to anger his wife.

"Okay." When his task was finished, he handed the offering to Stephen. "Done. Now talk."

Stephen's wife walked in, baby on hip, wearing a robe. She'd be all of five foot two if she had heels on. She was pretty, blonde. Her gaze bounced from the floor to Reed, and then to her husband. "What's going on? Why is he here in the middle of the night?"

This was all wrong. The house. The wife. The baby. What in hell's kitchen was going on?

"Here you go, honey." Stephen handed her the bottle. "It involves an active case, so I can't talk about it. But I'll be in bed before you put the baby down."

She took the bottle. The crying baby immediately settled the second he tasted milk. Warmth flooded Reed and his heart stirred.

He shook off the momentary weakness, attributing

it to the fact that yesterday had been the anniversary of his planned wedding with Leslie. Her betrayal had come the month before. Infidelity had a way of changing people's courses.

Kiera eyed her husband for a long moment then, on her tiptoes, kissed his cheek. "Don't be too long."

He bent down and kissed her forehead before planting another on his baby's cheek.

Her gaze narrowed when it landed on Reed. "I suspect you know how to use a door to get out?"

"Yes, ma'am." A moment of embarrassment hit. He'd acted on facts. He refused to wallow in guilt if he'd been wrong. Too many lives were at stake.

When she was safely out of earshot, Stephen continued, "Shane put me up to calling you. Said he needed your help on a case he was working, and that I should call you to see if I could take over for you. Said you were working on a routine immigration case."

"Shane Knox? He sure didn't let me in on it."

"Why would he do that?" Stephen's gaze was full of accusation now.

The weight of the conversation sat heavy on Reed's chest. "Because he's dirty."

"Hold on. That's a serious accusation. What makes you think that's the case?"

"I know."

"Then you need to fill me in."

Reed lifted the ball cap to reveal the bandage on his forehead. "Minutes after you made that call I was shot at before being run off the road. My Jeep caught fire."

More fireworks had to be going off in Stephen's brain based on the intensity of his eyes. "What happened to your witness?"

"She's in the hospital, but she'll be okay. The wreck was bad, but she'd been beaten up pretty badly before then."

"And Knox is connected to the initial incident?"

"As far as I know." Reed studied Stephen. "You called. I was run off the road."

"If they were coming after you, why have me call?" He snaked his fingers through his hair. "Never mind. I know. He was hoping to have her handed over to me. But why? I wouldn't have turned her over to him."

"He must've planned to follow you to the handoff so he could find us. He'd already sent men hunting for me, I'm sure of that."

"We traded vehicles a couple of weeks ago. He still has a few things in there. Must've left something in there he can track. Or he figured I wouldn't be suspicious if he stopped me somewhere along the way. You'd be leery after what you've been through. Or, maybe he planned to run me off the road instead."

"They want her alive. She has passwords to a computer. Or at least they think she does, which no longer matters because whether she produces them or not, they'll kill her." Reed rubbed the scruff on his chin. Dueño had gone to great lengths to hide his identity. Emily was the only person on the outside who'd heard his voice or could prove his existence. There was no doubt in his mind she'd been marked for death. The phone in his pocket vibrated. He fished it out and checked the text. As he made a run for the door, he said, "Something's going down at the hospital."

"Which one?" Stephen opened a drawer and pulled out an AR-15.

"ClearPond Hospital on I-45." Reed bolted out the door.

Stephen followed. "Then you're going to need backup."

"I appreciate it." Luke's message said the lights had gone out on the sixth floor, Emily's floor. Luke was smart enough to see it for what it was. But was Emily strong enough to move?

Without selling his brother short, Reed figured it'd be difficult to haul her away and fight off whoever had decided to breach the building.

He cursed Knox as he hopped into his brother's truck and fired up the engine, grateful for the help loading into the passenger's side.

Reed couldn't allow himself to consider the possibility that he wouldn't make it back to the hospital in time.

Chapter Eight

The door opened to Emily's room. Blackness surrounded her. Even with her hand stuck out flat, directly in front of her face, she couldn't see it.

"I'm to your right," Luke whispered, touching her arm.

An officer identified himself, flashing a light on his face. "Hospital security wants to move her to another room. They've established a safe route for us."

Luke squeezed her arm, but said nothing.

"Okay," she agreed.

"We'll unhook you from these machines to make it easier to transport you, okay?" the nurse said as she brushed against Emily's other side.

The beam of light transferred to her, and Emily saw fearful eyes.

"Sounds good. Do I have time to get dressed?"

"I'm afraid n—"

"She does," Luke interrupted, handing her a folded stack. "I brought fresh clothes."

As the tubes were unhooked, one by one, Emily pulled on a pair of jeans that fit perfectly and a V-neck cotton shirt. Thankfully, they'd let her keep her bra and underwear on earlier, and the dark had shielded her.

"You're good to go. Be careful. Those first few steps can be tricky," the nurse said.

"I will. Thank you."

"I'll try to find you later," the nurse whispered so quietly Emily barely heard.

Something hard, made of metal, was pressed to her hand. It had to be a weapon of some sort from the nurse.

The door opened again and footsteps grew distant.

Standing, Emily leaned against Luke for support and took a few tentative steps.

"I gotcha. Don't worry. I won't let you fall," he said.

She wanted to warn Luke. The nurse wouldn't have given her a weapon unless she'd wanted Emily to be able to defend herself. The hospital had been informed about the need for tight security. This instrument was more than a warning.

"Ready, ma'am?" the officer asked.

"Yes." How could she get the message to Luke without broadcasting it?

"Then, follow me."

An occasional beam of light could be seen in front of them as they followed behind the officer.

Emily tugged at Luke's sleeve. He squeezed her arm in response. Good, he knew she wanted to communicate something to him. She placed the metal object in his hand. He took it, squeezed again.

The floor was calm. Too quiet. Where were the other patients? Nurses? How would Reed know where they'd been moved? She remembered Luke had sent a text to his brother earlier.

Fear of not knowing where Reed was or when he'd return sent icy chills down her back. And where did these guys plan to take her? Hadn't she overhead Reed telling his brother that they couldn't trust anyone?

At least she'd had a chance to rest. Her knees were less wobbly with every step. She was gaining her bearings. She'd be ready to fight. *Might have to be.*

The officer turned right, his flashlight illuminating a long hallway.

Luke urged her to veer left. Almost the second he dropped her hand, she heard a shuffle. Then a quiet thud. She couldn't yell for help or she'd alert everyone. She said a silent protection prayer instead.

When a hand gripped her arm, she bit down a yelp.

"It's me," Luke whispered, guiding her through the hallway in the dark.

Walking proved challenging, let alone navigating through the blackness all around them.

A little piece of her feared she'd never see Reed again. But now, all she could focus on was getting out of the building alive.

What if they didn't make it? Outside had more men, more danger, more risk. Even if they hid, and gave Reed a road map to find them, how would he get through?

A wave of hopelessness washed over her as pain ripped through her thighs. Moving hurt.

Commotion from behind caused her heart to skip a beat. She heard at least three voices firing words in Spanish.

"I don't know what happened. They were behind me one second, the next I was on the floor." The voice was familiar, the police officer.

If Dueño had locals in his pocket, how would she and Luke make it out of this building alive? The irony of being killed in a hospital where people were brought back from the jaws of death on a daily basis hit her hard. Who would take care of her mother when she needed help? What about her other siblings? Would anyone other than her boss even know she'd died? Would anyone care?

Jared would notice only if she didn't show for work Monday. Her mortgage company would figure out she wasn't keeping up with her payments after a month or two. Eventually, they'd foreclose. At least she existed on paper.

But would anyone *really* know she was gone? Would anyone miss her?

Suddenly, for the first time in her life, she felt an overwhelming urge to be with someone who cared, with Reed.

The probability he would be able to find them was low. Sure, they could text their location, but that didn't mean he'd get through the militia waiting in the parking lot or the hallway.

Luke stopped and turned, pausing for a moment. Then a door opened and he guided her inside to a corner where she eased down. Pain shot through her thighs. The room had to be small because she'd taken only a couple of steps. A supply room?

The door closed.

"We can hide here for a little while," Luke said. His phone appeared. He covered the screen with one hand, allowing enough light to figure out where they were and thumbed a text with the other.

"Where are we? Don't they lock these doors?" Her guess of being in a supply room was dead-on.

"Supply closet. The nurse handed me the key. I'm guessing she knew what was going on."

"Explains why she gave me the piece of metal, whatever that was."

"She tipped me off that the officer wasn't there to help. Came in handy when I subdued him."

"How so? I didn't see a thing."

"She whispered when she walked past me."

"I heard the officer's voice back there. I'm guessing he'll live."

"A bullet would've made too much noise." The calm practicality in his voice when talking about killing someone was a stark reminder she wasn't remotely connected to the world she knew or understood anymore.

The snick of a lock cut through the quiet. Luke squeezed her arm and then let go, presumably to ready his weapon.

"Don't shoot. It's me. I was your floor nurse."

"How did you get in? I thought you gave Luke your key," Emily said.

"I'm the floor supervisor. I have a spare. Besides, when I noticed the men talking to the officer, I knew something was suspicious."

"Ever think about changing professions?" Luke asked. "You'd make a great cop."

"I'm addicted to all those crime shows on TV." She snickered quietly then suppressed it. "Figured you might need some help."

"Believe me, it's appreciated. And, believe me, I'm glad you're on my side."

"I hoped I'd find you in here. An officer pulled me away as soon as you left the room. I barely got away. Since I know the floor plan of the hospital, I had an advantage."

"I'm good there, too. Memorized it on the way in." His low voice didn't rumble the way his brother's did. Nor did it have the same effect on Emily.

There was something special about Reed Campbell. Being with him made her feel different in ways she couldn't begin to explain, let alone understand.

Would she live long enough to find out where it might go?

REED GRABBED AN extra Kevlar vest and told Stephen to take it. "My brother has the witness in a supply room on the sixth floor. He thinks they're safe. For now."

"No one knows what I look like. I can go first. Blaze a trail."

"On my last count, there were half a dozen men on the perimeter. That number could be double by now," Reed said flatly.

"How long have you been gone?"

"Hour and a half, max."

"Hopefully, the numbers haven't changed much."

The picture of Stephen's wife holding his baby popped into Reed's thoughts. All he had to worry about was himself. He didn't have a wife and child depending on him to come home every night. If anything happened to Reed, of course his family would miss him, but that wasn't the same thing by a long shot. Leslie had begged him to think about changing professions once they were married. And Reed had been dumb enough to consider it. "On second thought, this might be too dangerous. You stay here. I'll call if I need backup."

Stephen muttered the same curse word Reed had thought a second earlier. "This is my job. I do this for a living. What's the big deal?"

"I can think of two good reasons not to send you into what might be a death trap."

"Kiera knows who I am," he said, indignant.

"I don't know. It's risky. Even if I can breach the building, I have no idea what's waiting for me once I make it to the sixth floor. These guys are no joke, either. They probably have more guns than we do."

"Are you saying this mission is too dangerous for me, but the jobs we go out and do every single day aren't? That working for Border Patrol is a walk in the park?" Stephen issued a disgusted grunt as he shot daggers with his glare.

"It does seem ridiculous when you put it like that. You ever think about quitting? About getting a nine-to-five so you can watch your kid grow up?" Reed ran through a few best-case scenarios in his mind as they talked.

"My son is fine. I have every plan to be right there alongside my wife to see him off to college and beyond, but this is what I do. It's who I am. If my wife doesn't have a problem with it, then you sure as hell shouldn't."

Good point. "She never asks you to quit?"

"Why would she? She knew who I was when she married me." The look of disgust widened with his eyes.

Shock didn't begin to cover Reed's reaction. Everything Stephen had said was absolute truth, but Leslie had seen things very differently. She'd begged Reed to reconsider his line of work. Even said she didn't think they could have children as long as he was an agent. Her internet search hadn't done him any favors, either.

Yes, Border Patrol agents had the most dangerous jobs in law enforcement. Reed had calculated the risk when he took the job and had decided he could live with the odds. If he'd gone into Special Forces operations, the danger would've been greater. He figured most women would react the way Leslie had, so he gave up on getting serious for a while.

Good thing most women weren't like Leslie. They probably didn't cheat, either.

Reed put his hands up in the universal sign of surrender. "Sorry. I got no problem standing behind you, next to you, in front of you, whatever. I just don't want to go to sleep at night for the rest of my life with your kid's face being the last thing I remember."

Stephen issued a grunt. "You have a better chance of getting shot than I do. These ass-hats aren't even looking for me."

"True. If you're good with the risk, then I am, too. Besides, I need your help." Reed pulled into the gas station across the street from the hospital and cut his lights. He studied the building. It was the middle of the night, so it was unlikely there would be a shift change. The cafeteria wouldn't be open, either. No way to slip in unnoticed there. Security would be tight, as well. Then there were corrupt local police to deal with if he and Stephen got inside. The sixth floor would be crawling with Dueño's men. "You got any binoculars in your pack?"

"Yeah. Night vision." He pulled his gym bag from the backseat, dug around in it and produced a pair.

Reed surveyed the parking lot. Dueño's men had to be swarmed inside because there were only two left outside. From the looks of things, getting inside the building wasn't going to be the problem. Once there, Reed figured they'd be up against a wall. Almost all of Dueño's men were most likely on the sixth floor—which was the same place Luke and Emily were.

The need to see Emily, to make sure she was okay, seeded deep in the pit of his stomach. A primal instinct to protect her gripped him. Strange that they'd only just met.

After his relationship with Leslie, Reed Campbell

didn't *do* feelings while working this job. Leslie had taught him not to expect more than a casual relationship. He'd convinced himself that one day the adrenaline would no longer be enough to satisfy him and he'd get tired of the job or burned out on the demands. When that happened, he could change careers and could settle down. Having both at the same time seemed as out of reach as finding Cal and bringing him to justice.

Even more surprising was a woman who got it, who supported her husband and his career. Surely, Kiera was one of a kind.

Either way, Emily's case was about to get a lot more interesting. "You have a pen and paper in the bag?"

"Sure. Hang on." Stephen produced the items.

Reed sketched the hospital's layout. It was shaped like a T, the front doors being at the intersection. "Emily's room is here on the sixth so the supply closet must be nearby." He circled a spot on the map he'd drawn to the left of where the letter T most intersected. "So, there are two out here that we know of. No big deal there. Inside, there are at least four armed men, plus whoever else has joined the party that we don't know about. Another pair of local officers who might be dirty round out the guest list. Did I forget anyone?"

"That about sums it up based on what you've said so far. On our side, we have the two of us and your brother who's in the FBI, and he's with the witness?"

"You good with that?"

"I've worked in worse situations," Stephen said honestly.

Having backup was nice. Different. In their line of work, they didn't get that luxury most of the time. Only problem was they hadn't worked together before. Teams required teamwork, and that required people who knew the ins and outs of how each other worked. "No matter what we find in there, I'll always go right."

"Good. I like taking the left side. It's natural for me." Stephen pulled a Kevlar vest from his pack. "Looks like I'll need this."

"Ready?" Reed looked into Stephen's eyes, really looked, for any signs of hesitation.

The slightest delay in judgment and they'd both be dead. And that was most likely why Reed didn't choose a job in law enforcement working with a partner. He'd stand side by side with either of his brothers any day. But his future in another man's hands? *Not his warm-and-fuzzy.*

The black sky was dotted with tiny bursts of light. Highway noise pierced the otherwise quiet night.

Pitch-black covered the sixth floor. The rest of the hospital had lights.

Head down, gun palmed, Reed stalked toward the white building. He stopped at the edge of the parking lot, near the ER. A distraction would be nice right now, but Reed had never been able to rely on luck. Figured it was the reason he'd learned to work hard instead.

Tightening his grip on the butt of his Glock, he tucked his chin to his chest and quickened his stride toward the entrance. Stephen stayed back until Reed reached the glass doors. He took a position inside the building, and surveyed the lot. His buddy easily made it inside. It was all too easy. Then again, these guys were focused on Emily and they must believe they had her right where they wanted her. Plus, Luke could pass for Reed to the untrained eye.

The fact security was loose in the lot most likely meant

these jerks figured they had who they wanted trapped upstairs. It also indicated the closer Reed got to Emily and Luke, the more men there'd be to get past.

"Which way?" Stephen asked, inclining his chin toward the elevator, then the stairs.

"Both make too much noise. Plus, the light will give us away."

Out of better options, Reed pitched toward the stairs with Stephen close behind.

Reed stopped on the fifth floor. The only distraction he could count on would be one he created himself. The nurses' station was quiet save for the click of fingers on a keyboard. The young nurse glanced up. "Can I help you?"

Reed pointed to the badge clipped to his waistband.

She nodded. "I need to talk to my supervisor."

"Understood." He located a fire extinguisher and slammed it into the glass, sounding the alarm.

"Sir, you can't do that." The nurse burst from her chair, shouting over the wail of alarms.

Reed and Stephen made a play for the stairs. Within two steps of freedom, the door blasted open and two men in security uniforms blocked the entry.

"Step aside. We work for Border Patrol and we need to gain access to the stairwell." He motioned toward his badge.

The sound of feet shuffling in the stairwell broke through the noise as security stepped aside and allowed Reed through.

A gunshot split the air.

Must have come from behind.

"You good?" Reed asked.

"Yeah. You?"

A quick scan revealed Reed had not been hit. "Fine."

He took the stairs three at a clip. The stairwell would be full of people in another few seconds. Doors already opened and closed on lower levels. Panicked voices echoed.

If Reed were lucky, the men would scatter, too. He almost laughed out loud. *Luck?* Right. Go with that, he thought wryly. His best-case scenario? The commotion would give Luke a chance to escape with Emily.

Reed trusted his brother. So, why did he want to be the one to take Emily to safety?

Chapter Nine

Alarms pierced through the supply closet. Emily didn't dare cover her ears for fear she'd miss out on critical instructions.

"We need to move. Can you stand up?" Luke offered a hand.

"I'm good." She wouldn't tell him how much her body ached already.

"She needs to take it easy," the nurse said. "Think you can get us off this floor?"

"I have to," Luke said.

"Then I can get us out of here safely."

"How do we know Reed's okay?" Thirty minutes had passed since Emily had watched Luke text his brother with no response.

"Because of that sound." He motioned toward the air.

Reed had set off the fire alarm? She didn't want to acknowledge the relief flooding her, giving her the extra will to push forward.

"I'll go first. Squeeze my arm if you get in trouble," Luke whispered over the noise.

"Okay."

The door creaked open. Emily's breath caught in her

throat. She eased a few steps forward, one hand on the nurse and the other on Luke.

Even in the dark, she could see the silhouette of two men moving toward them. Her eyes had somewhat adjusted. She squeezed Luke's shoulder.

As the pair neared, she could make out a face. Reed's.

Ignoring the shivers running up her arms, she reached for him.

"We managed to scatter them, but not for long," he said. The rich timbre of his voice settled over her as he wrapped an arm around her waist for support.

He nodded toward his brother and took more of her weight as the nurse led them through a couple of back rooms and into a staff elevator.

"You're bleeding. What happened?" Emily touched the soaked spot on his sleeve.

"It's not from me." Reed double-checked himself as though unsure.

"Then who?" Emily asked.

Reed's gaze shot straight to the friend he'd brought with him. "They got you?"

"It's nothing." He lifted his shirt on his left side. "Just a flesh wound."

"Dammit, it's more than that." In a razor-sharp tone, he muttered the same curse Emily thought.

"Don't worry. I can take care of him. You two need to get out of here." The nurse pulled off her scrubs and handed her top to Emily. "Put this on."

"I can't leave my buddy." The anguish in his voice softened the earlier tension.

"You don't have a choice. Take her with you. I'll stay with him," Luke said.

"I—"

"When that door opens, I want both of you the hell out of here. We'll catch up as soon as…" His gaze searched Reed's friend.

"Stephen—"

"I'll catch up as soon as he's square," Luke finished. "I won't let anything else happen to him, I swear."

Emily eased the scrubs over her head with Reed's help. The tenderness in his touch warmed her. She tried her best to ignore it, considering they were about to face a parking lot full of Dueño's men—men who were trying to kill her.

"They'll be watching for her. All the exits will be covered," Reed said.

"Exactly why I'll pretend to be her. I'll hold on to these two and fake a limp," the nurse said.

Emily didn't want to put others in jeopardy for her sake. She remembered the nurse talking about her younger brother on his freshman spring break trip to Matamoros, Mexico, being ritualistically killed and buried. The emotion had still been raw in her voice after three years. Was that the reason she was intent on helping? "I still don't think this is a good idea."

The statement was met with nods of agreement from the men in the elevator.

"I understand why you have hesitations. I do. Seems like I'm putting myself out there for strangers. But I need to do this for Brian. I don't expect you to understand. Please don't stop me." The determination in her tone caused Emily to cave.

"These aren't the same men," Emily protested, but she already knew she'd lost the battle. Because she did understand the need to make things right for something in the past.

"They are in a sense. Those men are cut from the same cloth. They hurt innocent people and destroy lives." She paused a beat. "It's too late for me to help my brother, but I can help you. Don't take that away from me."

The moment of silence in the elevator said no one would argue.

Reed slipped off his Kevlar vest and placed it on the nurse before turning to Emily. The brilliance in his brown eyes pierced through her. "Think you can walk on your own through the parking lot?"

"I'll make it." She ignored the shivers trailing up her spine.

Reed bear-hugged his brother and then Stephen before turning to the nurse. "I'd be even more in your debt if you'll promise to take good care of this guy once you get out of here."

If the nurse didn't, Emily knew without a doubt that Reed wouldn't be willing to walk away. He'd take Stephen with him.

An emotion Emily couldn't quite pinpoint hit her fast and hard. She'd never known that kind of loyalty before. At the House, people would drop in and out based on their own needs. No one seemed concerned with the children other than making sure they had food and clothing. Schedules made people slaves, the guy in charge had said, so there was no routine.

Homeschooling had been inconsistent, too. In addition to a couple of workbooks, the children had been given homemade pamphlets on the importance of peace and love. Emily appreciated both and yet there was no real love at the House. No one had been there at the end of the day to tuck her into bed and make her feel secure as her father had when she was little. No one had taken her to the playground to be with other kids, since leaving the compound was forbidden. No one had nursed her cuts and bruises or held her while she cried herself to sleep. All of which had happened too often in the House, and especially in the early years when she was trying to adjust to her new life.

Busying herself with the little kids had been a much-needed de-stressor. Work had a way of providing a welcomed distraction. Was she still hiding behind hers?

The elevator dinged, indicating they'd reached the bottom floor. Tension billowed out as the doors opened.

Reed took Emily's hand, palm to palm, as they stepped out of the elevator. "Ready?"

"I hope." Contact with Reed seemed to shrink the world to the two of them. Emily prayed she'd be prepared for whatever waited ahead, in her immediate future and beyond.

Scrubs made quite a difference in helping Emily blend in. They did nothing to help her walk faster. She had to be in severe pain to stand straight, let alone move. Frustration nipped at Reed.

He had two choices if he wanted to move faster: leave Emily alone for a few minutes in the parking lot to bring the truck to her, or carry her. Leaving her unguarded even for a second wasn't a real consideration, which left carrying her. There was no doubt he could easily hoist her over his shoulder. But could he pick her up and get her to the truck without drawing attention? At least the false alarm had brought people out of the hospital. Standing around in small groups, they provided a buffer between Emily and him and Dueño's men.

Stephen had a bullet scrape to prove how far they'd go to stop them.

A fresh wave of guilt followed by red-hot anger pulsed through him at letting his buddy get shot. Reed would have to face Kiera and her baby to explain and apologize for what had happed. No way would he sleep at night otherwise.

Worrying about a wife and child, even Stephen's, was a distraction Reed couldn't afford when his mind needed to be sharp. Maybe Leslie had been right. A man in this job had no right to put his wife and child through the pain of not knowing if he'd be coming home. Or, if he did, what kind of shape he'd be in. And yet, a little piece of him wanted to believe things would be different if Emily was the one he'd be coming home to.

Small crowds stood, facing the building. Others walked slowly to their vehicles, checking back often. They'd hide Emily's pace as long as Reed mimicked them. He did.

"Slow and steady. Take your time." The feel of her hand in his warmed him in places he shouldn't allow. And yet, it felt so natural to touch her.

The kiss they'd shared earlier wasn't helping his concentration, either.

Distractions he couldn't afford fired all around him when she was this close. Being away from her was even worse.

They made it to the edge of the lot without drawing attention.

He and Emily were safe for now. Part of him was relieved beyond measure. The other part didn't like putting his friend and brother in harm's way.

Once clear of the lot, he'd check in with his brother

while he located a decent hotel. Emily needed a good night of sleep.

Reed wrapped his arm around her waist and took most of her weight. "I can carry you if it'll help."

"We made it this far. I can go a few more yards. I just hope they're all right."

"As soon as they realize they're after the wrong people, they'll circle back to the hospital." He helped her into the truck.

"I hope we're long gone before that happens," she said through a yawn, the medicine obviously doing its job.

"I plan to be. Try to get some rest." He nodded toward his shoulder.

"I doubt I can after all that." She slid across the seat as he belted himself, and leaned against him.

"Close your eyes. You might be surprised at how tired you are." He started the engine and eased the truck onto the highway.

"How far away is the place we're staying?"

"About twenty minutes up the road."

"Now that you mention it, I could use a bed to stretch out on even if I don't sleep."

Sleep was about the last thing Reed could imagine with Emily curled up next to him. He was in dangerous emotional territory with her because he could imagine sleeping next to her, or better yet not sleeping, for the foreseeable future. "You're brave. I'm proud of what you did back there."

She smiled one of her light-the-sky-with-brilliance smiles.

Not five minutes into the drive she drifted off to sleep, her soft, even breathing not more than a whisper in his ear.

Her being with him was the only thing that made sense.

And yet, what did he really know about her?

They'd barely met, he reminded himself for the twentieth time as he looked out at the long stretch of highway in front of him. And yet, he couldn't deny the familiarity she'd talked about earlier—closeness he felt just as strongly as she did even if he wasn't quite ready to acknowledge it as special.

It was special.

The sign for his exit came up. Reed put on his blinker and changed lanes. The movement caused Emily to stir. He stilled as he took the off-ramp, afraid to move too much so he wouldn't hurt her. She burrowed into his side and mewled softly.

Damn, that sound was the sexiest thing he'd heard in a very long time, which pretty much proved the well had been bone-dry for him. What did it say about him that every time she was near his thoughts were inappropriate?

She sat up straight and rubbed her eyes, blinking against the sudden light from the highway. "Are we there?"

"Yes." He heard how thick and raspy his own voice had become. A ride in a truck shouldn't qualify as the sexiest moment of his year. So far, it did.

Reed vowed to change that once this case was over.

"A bed sounds amazing right now."

"Stay here while I grab a key from the hotel desk."

Within minutes, he returned and helped her inside.

Standing in front of the door, he jammed the keycard inside the slip. His effort was met with a red light. He muttered a curse, and then an apology. A couple of more tries yielded the same result.

"I think you have to pull out faster."

Reed wasn't about to touch that statement. "Would you like to try? I don't seem to have the right touch."

"Sure," she said with a coy smile.

He moved to the side and allowed her access. The damn thing lit green before she slid the card out.

"See how it's done?"

Suppressing a grin, he helped her inside, where a plush king-size bed filled the room.

"What's that smile all about?"

"Not going there." He chuckled about all the other things he'd like her to show him. Joking was his way of easing the tension from what had happened earlier.

He immediately texted Luke to get a read on Stephen's condition.

With Luke behind the wheel, they'd gotten rid of the men who'd chased them. Stephen was doing fine.

Relief flooded Reed. He turned to Emily, who was studying his expression.

"Did you get good news?"

"Stephen's grumbling about not needing a nurse, but he's cooperating. And he'll be fine. He and Luke are going to bunk at the nurse's place tonight."

"She's a good woman. We wouldn't have survived without her."

"Agreed. On both counts." He stopped in front of the bathroom door. "You want me to run a bath for you?"

"The nurse helped me shower at the hospital. I'm all clean."

There was an image Reed didn't need in his head. Plus, the smell of flowery soap was still all over her. He tried to shake it off. Didn't help. He settled her onto the bed, trying to suppress the smirk stuck to his lips.

"Okay, what's going on?"

"Nothing I can talk about."

"Why not?" Her gaze moved from his eyes to his lips, where it lingered, then down his body.

Scratch what he'd thought a little while ago. That was the sexiest thing to happen to him in the past year. "I need a shower."

"Want some help?" she teased.

"Normally I'd take you up on that." He stalked across the room, pausing at the door to the bathroom.

"I was kidding. No man on earth would want to shower with me the way I must look."

He moved to the bed and leaned over her, stopping a fraction of an inch before their lips touched. "Why not? Most men I know appreciate a beautiful woman."

Those stunning hazel eyes of hers darkened. Being this close was probably a bad idea. Even if she wasn't his witness, she was injured. No way could they do anything in her condition.

Autopilot had kicked in, and Reed couldn't stop himself from reaching out to touch her face. He ran his finger gently along the line of her jaw, and then her lips.

Her hands came up around his neck, and her fingers tunneled into his hair.

Kissing her would be another bad idea, but that knowledge didn't stop him, either.

Softly, he pressed his lips to hers, careful not to hurt her. She tasted sweet and hot, and a little like peppermint, most likely a remnant of brushing her teeth at the hospital. But mostly, she tasted forbidden. A random thought breezed through that he shouldn't be doing this. His sense of right and wrong should have him pulling away. Where was his self-discipline?

Tell that to his stiff length.

Better judgment finally won out when he realized this was about as smart as jabbing his hand into a pot of hot oil. Even if she wasn't his witness, they couldn't finish.

Reed pulled back. The look of surprise in her eyes caused his resolve to falter. "I can't keep going. Not comfortably."

"Oh." She sounded confused.

"Believe me. I want to." How should he put this? It wasn't his nature to be delicate.

"Oh?"

"I don't want to risk anything with your injuries."

The look in her eyes, the hurt, almost had him changing his mind. She looked away. "I understand. It's probably for the best."

"Can I take a rain check?"

"You don't have to say that to make me feel better. I kissed you in the hospital. Not the other way around. I understand that you're not attracted to me."

That's what she thought? "Do you want to know what you do to me?"

She didn't respond.

"I'm going in the other room to take a shower and quite possibly take matters into my own hands because I want you so badly right now, it's painful." He glanced down at his straining zipper.

She did, too.

"Oh. Sorry about that." Her cheeks flushed six shades past red, causing his heart to stir and bringing an amber glow to her already bright face.

"Don't be embarrassed. I'm not. One thing you can count on from me is honesty. If we're going to spend time together, I expect the same."

He was rewarded with a warm smile. Emily was outdoors, warmth and open skies with a sexual twist. And as long as she was willing, he had every intention of showing her just how desirable she was when he could be absolutely sure he wouldn't be hurting her in the process.

"Honesty is a good thing," she finally said. She winked, and it made her eyes glitter. "And as long as we're being honest, I can help you with that little problem in the shower."

"One time won't be enough for me." He stood and walked toward the bathroom, stopping at the door. "And it's not little."

Chapter Ten

Reed finished drying himself, brushed his teeth and slipped into a clean pair of boxers. He climbed under the covers on the opposite side of the bed so he wouldn't wake Emily. She'd left one of the bedside table lamps on, and it cast a warm glow over the room. He doubted he'd be able to grab any shut-eye for himself, but she needed her rest.

As he settled in for a night of nonsleep, she shifted and threw her leg over his. His pulse kicked up a notch or two. Heck, it raised more than he wanted to admit.

Yeah, he definitely wouldn't be getting any sleep now. Not with her silky warm skin pressed to his. How could his thigh touching hers be so damn sexy?

She reached across his bare chest, only a thin piece of cotton stopping her firm breast from touching his bare skin. He groaned. It was going to be a long night.

He was aroused. She was fast asleep. Even if she was wide awake, it didn't change the fact that she was badly injured.

That she'd taken off everything but a T-shirt and underwear brought his erection back to life with a vengeance.

His whole body stiffened. He didn't want to move for fear he'd hurt her.

And then he felt her hands moving over his chest.

"You can't break me," she whispered, and her voice slid over him, warming him. Her hands moved across his chest, stopping at the dark patch of hair in the center.

He was afraid he'd do just that. Hurt her. So he wouldn't force anything. Her mouth found his, and her tongue slid inside.

His hands moved, too, with gentle caresses as he smoothed his palm across the silken skin of her stomach.

She moaned as he cupped her breast. She carefully re-positioned, a reminder they needed to take it slow, and his sex pressed to her stomach.

Last thing Reed needed to think about just now was her light purple panties. He already knew they were silk. With an image like that and her curled against him, things would end before they even started. She seemed to want this every bit as much as he did. Used to being in charge in bed, he'd have to remember to let her be in control.

Lying side by side, Reed slowly lifted her shirt as he bent down then slicked his tongue over her nipple. It hardened to a peak. The soft mewling sound she made stiffened his length. Much more of this and he'd be done right then and there. Her back arched then the sound she made next stopped him in his tracks.

"Are you okay?"

"Y-es." The way she drew out the word told him she wasn't convinced.

There was a point of no return when it came to fore-play, and a breast in his mouth had always been the line for him. They'd careened sideways and beyond as far as Reed was concerned, so stopping now would prove even more difficult. Except when it came to pain. No way could he feel good about having sex if it hurt his partner in any way. And the painful groan that had just passed her lips had the effect of a bucket of cold water being poured over him.

"We can't do this." He gently extracted himself from in between her thighs because one wriggle of those taut hips and he'd be in trouble again.

She didn't put up an argument this time.

Reed settled onto his back as she curled around his left side. "Tell me where it hurts."

"This position is good. The other way only hurt when I moved." She laughed. It was the kind of laugh that promised bright sunshine and blue skies.

He leaned over and pressed a kiss to her forehead.

"You make me happy," she said in a sexy, sleepy voice.

Reed should be coming up with a strategy for how they were going to catch the guys chasing them instead of feeling perfectly contended to lie in bed with Emily in his arms. But that's exactly what was happening. And he wished they could stay there for a while. Except that wasn't an option. They'd have to leave first thing in the morning. "Me, too, sweetheart. Think you can get some rest? We have a long day ahead tomorrow."

She blinked up at him with those pure, honest hazel eyes. "What will you do if I go to sleep?"

"Come up with a plan."

"I want to help."

"The best thing you can do for either of us is rest."

It didn't take fifteen minutes for the medicine to overtake her willpower and for her to fall asleep again.

Reed wasn't so lucky. He ran through several scenarios, none of which gave him a warm-and-fuzzy feeling. Then there was the thought of visiting Stephen's wife. Why did it weigh so heavily on Reed's conscience?

A text message from Luke had confirmed that Stephen was fine. His injury wasn't more than a big scrape, a flesh wound. The trio had made it out of the parking lot without too much trouble as had Reed and Emily. His assumption that the men who'd followed them would give up after they realized they were following the wrong people had turned out to be true.

Then there was the issue of Emily to think about. Her warmth as she pressed against him while she slept. He could get used to this.

EMILY STRETCHED AND blinked her eyes open to a quiet room and an empty bed. The mattress was cold where Reed used to be.

Where was he?

Climbing out of the bed brought a few aches and stiff muscles to life. Surprisingly, some of her pain had subsided. She moved to the bathroom, brushed her teeth and dressed.

Back in the room, she noticed his keys and cell phone were missing. She prayed nothing had happened in the middle of the night to make him leave, such as getting a hot lead.

The thought of Reed being out there, alone, with Dueño's men surrounding him tightened a coil in her chest. Surely, he wouldn't go anywhere near them without someone to back him up.

Moving to the window to peek outside, she heard the snick of the lock and froze.

Reed shuffled in with company. She recognized his brother, who was following closely behind. He glanced at the bed with a raised eyebrow.

Emily let out the breath she'd been holding.

"I brought breakfast," Reed said with a forced smile. "How are you this morning?"

"Much better." She took the brown bag and inhaled the scent of breakfast tacos. "Smells amazing."

Reed slid his arm around her waist as he moved beside her. With his touch, heat fizzed through her body. Too bad they had company.

He helped her to the desk.

"Is something wrong? What happened?" Emily tried to brace herself for more bad news. "Is Stephen okay?"

"Yeah. He'll be fine. The nurse bandaged him up at her place last night."

"That where you two spent the night?" She picked a breakfast taco out of the bag and unwrapped it, keeping one eye on Reed.

"Yeah. Her house isn't far from here. She gave Stephen a ride home this morning, so I asked Reed to pick me up."

She set her breakfast taco down and turned to Reed. "Then what's going on?"

"Luke has to get back to North Texas for a case he's working on. He'll take us to a car my boss has stashed for us and then you and I will have to take it from there." Reed took a breakfast taco and then handed the bag to his brother.

The thought of leaving the relative safety and comfort of the hotel held little appeal. However, staying meant they couldn't follow leads. Besides, wasn't there a saying about sitting ducks? It was probably better to keep on the move. "When do we head out?"

"After we eat," Reed said, taking a seat next to her.

Emily finished her food and then excused herself to the bathroom, stopping in front of the mirror. Even as a teenager, she'd resisted the urge to go blonde. Now she was living proof it was a bad idea. With her hazel eyes, the lighter shade washed her out. Grateful to have real clothing and a rubber band, she pulled her hair up in a ponytail and washed her face. Some of the swelling had gone down, and her bruises were already yellowing. The sunburn had improved dramatically. The peeling was easing up, too.

Her eyes had seen better days, and she wished she had makeup, but other than that she figured nothing had happened that would leave a permanent mark so far.

Circumstances weren't good. Thinking about being broke and totally dependent on someone else didn't sit well. Even though Reed had proved he could be trusted. He'd kept by her side and put his own life on the line to save her, which wasn't the same as needing him more than she needed air.

If men hadn't started shooting at them, would Reed have hauled her in and walked away, though?

None of that mattered now. Second-guessing the situation wouldn't help. Reed Campbell was a good man who was doing what he believed to be the right thing. She respected him for it.

Even so, Emily wanted her own money, her own car and her own clothes. The only way to get those things was to convince Reed to take her to her town house, which was risky.

Looking at her reflection, it was readily apparent she wouldn't get by on her good looks. She almost laughed out loud. How could anyone get past her current condition? And hadn't Reed seemed to look past all that and see her from the inside?

Hadn't he said that they felt close because they'd survived a near-death experience? And that was most likely true because she'd never believed in love at first sight.

Even if she did, no way would she trust it. Relationships grew by getting to know someone. Sure, what she felt for him was different. Special, even. But real love? Her heart said it was possible, but her mind shut down the thought.

Rather than jump into that sinkhole feetfirst, Emily decided to hold whatever else she felt at bay. Yes, she was physically attracted to Reed. There was no denying it, especially with how right she felt in his arms. Crazier still, he seemed to return the sentiment.

She'd be smart to exercise caution, and not get too caught up in emotions that could change in an instant.

Her mom had loved her dad with everything inside her. Look what had happened there. Emily had trusted her father. Look where that had gotten her. She'd tried to save her mother with similar results.

And the last serious relationship she'd gotten involved in? The jerk turned out to be married with kids. Emily had spent last year's vacation curled in a ball on her bed, crying. She'd pretty much acquiesced to the idea that even though her heart wanted things normal people had— white-picket fence, a husband, children—those "things" most likely weren't in the cards for her. She'd settled into the routine of work, free from distractions. With no real attachments, her weekends were free for overtime.

Even though it had been a year ago, being put in the role of other woman had been like a knife wound to her chest. Jack had said he respected her space and wanted to take it slow, for her sake. He was actually busy at his kids' soccer games and then date nights with his wife on the weekends.

Knowing Emily had done that to another woman, even if unintentionally, had left behind an invisible gash across her chest—a scar that might never heal.

Love hurt. Love was unfair. Love had consequences.

Was she falling in love with Reed? Whatever was happening, she'd never felt such an initial impact when she'd met someone before. It was like reentering the earth's atmosphere from space.

Since her heart wanted to plow full speed ahead, she would force some logic into the situation. When it came to Reed, caution was Emily's new best friend.

"Ready?" Reed called from the other room, forcing her attention out of her heavy thoughts.

"Might as well be." She took a last look in the mirror and followed them out the door.

They walked to the car with Reed in front and Luke behind her.

Luke took the driver's seat. Emily squeezed in the middle. Reed was to her right.

She reached for the seat belt and winced, pain shooting across her chest. Her bruised ribs had something to say about the movement.

"Here. Let me get that for you." Reed made a move to help.

"No, thanks. I can manage by myself." And she had every intention of keeping it that way.

Chapter Eleven

By the time they reached The Pelican, the doors had just opened for lunch. Reed shifted in his seat to get a better view, scanning the surrounding area on the two-lane highway. Palm trees lined the streets. Their relatively thin stalks made it difficult to hide behind, giving Reed a decent view of the scattered buildings next to open fields.

The lot to the restaurant was empty. Reed cracked the truck's window. The air outside had that heavy, middle-of-summer, salty-beach smell. They weren't close enough to the water to benefit from a cool ocean breeze. "The car should be parked around back if it hasn't been towed."

Gravel crunched underneath the tires as the truck eased through the parking lot and toward the twin Dumpsters behind the restaurant where a few cars were parked.

"I'll have to run inside to pick up the keys."

Luke backed the truck into a spot positioned in the corner so that they could see anyone coming from around the building. He shifted gears to Park, leaving the engine idling. "You want us to go in with you?"

"Nah. It's better if I go in alone. Fewer people will notice that way. You keep watch from here." Reed slid out of the truck and secured his cowboy hat. He fished his cell out of his pocket and held it up. "Let me know if anything looks suspicious."

"I'm on it."

Reed stuffed the cell in his front pocket, lowered the tip of his Stetson and tucked his gun in his holster. He took Emily's hand and squeezed. "You've been quiet for most of the ride. Are you hurting?"

"A little. Nothing I can't handle." She smiled but it didn't make her eyes sparkle like before when she'd looked at him.

He made a mental note to ask about that later, and turned to his brother. "I'm not out in two minutes, don't hesitate to come after me."

Luke nodded. "Grab that key and get your butt back here."

Reed's boots kicked up dust as he walked.

The hostess looked young, as if she might be home on summer break from college. She greeted him. "Table for one?"

"Men's room first?" He smiled, not really answering her question.

She pointed to where he already knew it was. He'd been in the restaurant once before with Gil.

This early, there were no other patrons. His boots scuffed along the sawdust-covered floors. Metal buckets filled with peanuts were being placed on the tables. A waiter was hovering next to a waitress as she filled an ice pail from the soda machine. Both were laughing. Judging by the way she flipped her hair and smiled, both were flirting, too.

Not much else was going on other than bottles of salt and pepper being filled and placed on tables. The usual prelunch-crowd preparations were being made.

Reed located the men's room and slipped inside, moving straight to the sink farthest from the urinals. He slid his hand under the porcelain rim and felt around for the key. There was nothing. He bent his knees and leaned back on his heels so he could visually scan underneath. Bingo. There it was. Reed palmed it, and headed out of the bathroom.

As he neared the front door, the hostess smiled. "Your table's ready."

"Change of plans." He smiled, and she blushed. Guess she was doing a little flirting herself. Normally, he'd enjoy the attention. It was barely a blip on his radar now, leaving him wondering if his lack of interest had something to do with his stress meter, or his growing attraction to Emily.

He fished his cell out of his pocket and hit Gil's name in the contacts. The call rolled into voice mail. Reed muttered a curse as he fired off a text, and moved toward his brother. Reed shrugged.

Luke kept visually sweeping the area as Emily slid out of the passenger side.

"Got it," Reed said.

Emily took the arm he offered.

Thoughts about her, how warm she felt curled up next to him last night, had no place distracting him. He helped her lean against the hood of the vehicle. He'd just pressed the unlock button when his phone rang.

Reed gripped the handle at the same time he heard a click from underneath the car. What would they have done? The car was there, so they must've wanted him to get inside.

Dropping to the dirt, he climbed around on all fours

until he saw it. Wires and metal were taped together to the underbelly of the car. A bomb. He'd most likely detonated it by lifting the handle. He needed to get Emily off the hood. "Get back in the truck."

"What's under there?" Her gaze widened.

"It's wired!" he shouted to Luke. Reed was to his feet and by Emily's side in two seconds, urging her forward. Not wanting to hurt her was outweighed by his fear of the bomb going off with both of them right there.

His brother said the same curse word Reed was thinking. As he rounded the side of the truck, time seemed to still. The explosion nearly burst his eardrums. The earth shook underneath his boots. The truck had shielded much of his body from shrapnel. He dropped to his knees, managing to maintain his hold on Emily. Her arms tightened around his neck and her head buried where his neck and shoulder met.

Luke was out of the truck, moving toward them. Reed had dropped his cell and so the connection with Gil had been lost. Without a doubt his boss would do everything in his power to protect Reed, so who the hell figured out where the car and key were? The only other person from the agency Reed had been in contact with was Stephen. No way could this have been Stephen's doing. He was clean. Besides, he didn't even know about the stashed car. Someone else had figured it out. But who?

Between Reed and Luke, they hoisted Emily onto the bench seat of the truck. If they'd been parked any closer to the car, Reed didn't want to think about what would've happened to them. Before he could finish asking Emily if she was okay, Luke had pulled a fire extinguisher from the back of his truck and blasted the cool foam toward the blaze.

"I'm okay. Just a little freaked out," Emily said. Her bravery shouldn't make him proud. It did.

"I've already notified the police. We'll need to stick around long enough to give a statement. Then we'll head back to Dallas." Luke maneuvered his jaw as though he were trying to pop the pressure in his ears, and tossed the empty canister into the Dumpster.

Ringing noises blocked most of Reed's hearing. "Can you set us up with a place to stay?"

"Sure thing. How about Gran's?"

"Thought about Creek Bend. Might be a good option given the circumstances."

"We can use my car if you'll take us to my town house," Emily said. Her vacant expression indicated she was in shock.

Luke glanced from Emily to Reed. He nodded. "Might be a good idea to see if they've already been there."

"I guess we'll find out, won't we?" Reed shrugged.

"Want to send Nick over to check it out while we're on the way?"

"Good idea. I'd hate to lose more time, and these guys seem to be a step ahead so far." The tide needed to turn. Reed was getting a little tired of being on the wrong end of the wave.

"How will he get inside without a key?" Emily asked. The answer seemed to dawn on her when her eyes lit up and she said, "Oh. Right. Guess he doesn't exactly need to use the door. Tell him my alarm code is six-one-five-three. There's a small window in the laundry room toward the back. It'll be easy to break in and slip through it. There's a huge shrub in front of it. That window is the reason I put in an alarm in the first place."

Luke's cell was already out before she finished her sentence.

A squad car roared into the lot, kicking up dust and gravel.

Another cop on Dueño's payroll? The thought crossed Reed's mind. Luke's clenched jaw said he feared the same. But they both knew logic dictated only one or two cops would be dirty on any given police force, so the odds were in Luke and Reed's favor. On the off chance the guy didn't walk on the right side of the law, the crowd that had gathered would deter him from doing anything stupid.

Cell phones were out recording the damage, which could bring on more trouble for him and Emily. Social media would soon light up with the account, and the chances of Dueño's men pinpointing Emily at this location grew by the second. Reed turned to where Emily sat in the truck. "Lie down and stay low until we get out of here."

That was the first thing on his agenda.

Luke instinctively moved in between the gathering crowd and Emily, blocking everyone's line of sight and therefore their ability to snap a picture of her.

Reed, keeping his hands out in the open in plain sight, stopped midway between the truck and the officer. The cops around here didn't see much gunfire, which made them itchy, a threat. They constantly prepared for the one-off chance something could go wrong. The nervous twitch this guy had was his biggest tell.

"My name's Reed Campbell and I work for Homeland Security in the US Border Patrol Division."

"Keep your hands where I can see them." The guy inched forward.

Reed kept his high, visible. "My badge is attached to my belt on my left hip."

"Stay right there. Whoever's in the truck, put your hands up and come out." The high pitch wasn't good.

Emily raised her hands and kept her head low.

"Sir, if you make her come out of that truck, you'll be putting her life in danger." Reed motioned toward the sea of cell phones recording the event.

The officer shouted at the crowd to put their phones away or be arrested.

"Your boss should have gotten a call from mine," Reed said.

The cop's radio squawked. He leaned his chin to the left side and spoke quietly. His tense shoulders relaxed, and he lowered his weapon. "My supervisor confirmed your identity, Agent Campbell. Sorry about before."

Reed shook the outstretched hand in front of him. "Not a problem. The woman in the truck is my witness. This is my brother Luke. He's FBI."

The officer's eyes lit up as he shook Luke's hand. Reed choked down a laugh. He'd be hearing about how the FBI was better than Border Patrol on the way to Plano for sure because of that one.

Firemen had arrived and were checking the scene. Luke had already pulled a fire extinguisher from the truck and put out the fire. Reed finished giving the officer his statement. He shook Luke's hand rather enthusiastically one more time before clearing a path for them so they could leave.

When they settled into the truck, Emily leaned her head on Reed's shoulder and closed her eyes.

They hadn't gone five miles before Luke fired the

first barb. "Told you the FBI is better. Take the cop, for instance. Did you see his reaction—"

"We both know more agents are killed in my line of work than yours," Reed shot back, grateful for a light-hearted distraction to ease the tension in the cab. "And I think we also know the officer had a professional crush on you."

"I can't help it if I'm good-looking, too," Luke said with his usual flicker of a smile. "And you're still there because?"

The circumstances might not be ideal, but Luke cracking jokes and smiling was a good thing. He'd gone far too long after his stint in the military in solitude, refusing to talk to anyone. Since reuniting with his ex-wife, signs of the old Luke were coming back. "We both know Julie's going to make you quit after the wedding."

"Look, baby bro, there's something I've been meaning to tell you." Luke's serious expression jumped Reed's heart rate up a few notches.

"Don't leave me hanging. Get on with it."

"Julie and I, well, since this wasn't our first time, we decided not to wait. We got married last weekend."

"And you didn't tell me?" Reed feigned disgust. In truth, he couldn't be happier for his brother.

"We didn't let anyone in on it. Headed over to the justice of the peace's office after thinking about everything. It's not like it was our first go, so we didn't want to make a big production. Seemed to make more sense to keep it about us."

Reed belted out a laugh.

"What's so funny about me getting married to my wife?"

"Well, that for starters."

Luke shook his head and chuckled. "Okay, you got me. That sounds messed up."

"You think?"

His brother's laugh rolled out a little harder this time. "Yeah, it's a lot screwed up. But we never should've divorced in the first place."

"That's the smartest thing you've said today." Reed thought for a second. Oh, this was about to get really good. "Holy crap. You said you haven't told anyone else yet?"

"No." The problem with that word seemed to occur to Luke a second after it left his mouth. "That's not going to go down well, is it?"

"Gran will not be amused."

"Maybe you should tell her. You know, soften the initial impact."

"Oh, hell no. I'm not risking my ears."

"You think there'll be a lot of yelling?"

"Yeah. There'll be a lot of that. Then, she'll tell you that you're not too old for a butt-whooping. This is going to be dramatic."

"You gotta help me out here. Tell her for me," Luke pleaded.

"I plan to be there when she's told. But I have no plans to step into that fire barefoot. Your best bet is to bring Julie with you."

"Good idea. Surely, Gran won't want to scare her off."

"No, that's a great idea. And you owe me one for that."

"Fine. Then, I'll help you tell everyone about your friend here."

Reed glanced at Emily, thankful she was sound asleep. Besides, how'd this turn into a discussion about her? "What's that supposed to mean?"

"I'm not stupid. I can see you have feelings for her."

"And?" Reed wasn't ready to talk about what he had with Emily, if anything. Hell, he hadn't figured it out for himself, yet.

"I'm only saying she's a sweet person. You could do a lot worse."

"She's my witness. This is an investigation." The finality in his words most likely wouldn't sell Luke on the idea, but Reed had to try.

"You sure that's all?" His brow was arched as he leaned his wrist on top of the steering wheel, relaxing to his casual posture again.

Was it? Hell if Reed knew.

"Whatever is or isn't happening between the two of you, I think you need to have a conversation with her about federal protection."

"What? You think I haven't already?" Reed sounded offended to his own ears. His shoulder muscles bunched up, tense. A weekend-long massage wouldn't untangle that mess.

"Oh. Sorry. I just assumed since she was still here that you hadn't brought it up."

"If it makes you feel any better, it was the first thing I mentioned to her. She doesn't want it."

"And you don't, either."

"Here we go again." This conversation didn't need to happen.

"You may have been the quiet one, but nothing's ever gotten in your way once you set your mind to it."

"I gave her the options. She turned them down. End of story. What else was I supposed to do?"

"Persuade her," Luke said without blinking. "You have

to have considered the fact it may be the only way to guarantee her safety."

"Believe me, I have."

"So, why didn't you convince her of that?"

What was with the riot act? "I did what I could. In case you haven't noticed, she's a grown woman capable of thinking for herself."

"I noticed. Half the men in the country would notice her, too. The other half would be afraid their wives would catch them staring with their mouths open. She's a knockout even in the condition she's in. The fact hasn't been lost on you."

"I'm neither blind nor an idiot. Get to your point." Of course he'd noticed how her full breasts fit perfectly in his hands. Her round hips and soft curves hadn't gotten past him, either. The imprint of her body pressed to his still burned where they'd made contact. He'd become rock-hard when she'd thrown her leg over his last night. Did he want to sleep with her? Yeah. Was it more than that? Had to be since Reed hadn't done casual sex since he'd been old enough to buy a lottery ticket. Didn't mean he had to think with his hormones.

Luke hesitated, as if he was choosing his next words carefully. "I know you're too smart to jeopardize a mission or a witness, so I won't insult you. Deciding to keep her with you might not be in her best interest. It's up to you to make her see that."

"I don't care where she is as long as she's safe," he lied. Reed didn't make a habit of deceiving his brothers, so part of him was surprised to hear the words coming out of his mouth. The truth was he did care. And Luke was right. Probably too much. Reed's agitation had more to do with the fact that his brother was forcing Reed to think about his feelings for Emily, which was not something he wanted to do. Not with cars exploding and danger around every corner. His mind needed to stay sharp, so he wouldn't miss a connection when the other guys made a mistake. Given enough time, they would screw up.

His cell pumped out his ringtone. He glanced at the screen, grateful for the distraction. "It's Nick."

"Hey, baby bro," Nick said.

"What'd you find?"

"The place is in good shape but someone's been here. Thankfully the codes are still taped under her desk, like she said."

"Have you contacted SourceCon's security team?"

"Yeah. They're cooperating. Of course, they want to handle their own investigation, but they've agreed to give us full access to their people."

"Good point. Maybe someone on the inside knows something."

The line beeped. Reed checked the screen. "My boss is calling, so I'll have to catch up with you later. Keep me posted on anything you find."

"Will do. Be safe, baby bro."

Reed said goodbye and switched to his other call. "What's the word, boss?"

"I got a rundown on what happened from the chief of police. I tried to call you earlier when we got cut off but my call went straight to voice mail. Didn't do good things to my blood pressure."

"I must've been out of range for cell service. There are a lot of dead spots out this way."

"At least you're all right."

That was the second time someone said that in the

past two minutes. "So far, so good. Someone wants this witness pretty badly."

"Clearly, they want you, too. I believe this case is also connected to yours."

"I know Stephen Taylor was set up by Shane Knox, but what does he have to do with me?"

"He was in the room when I spoke to you yesterday. He must've decoded our conversation and located the car." Anguish lowered Gil's baritone. "It's my fault this happened. I'm sorry that I trusted him."

"What's the connection, though? I don't remember Knox and Cal working together."

"I have their files right here in my hands. Turns out, they went to the same high school. Grew up in Browns-ville, Texas, together. Played football. To say they knew each other well is an understatement. As my teenage daughter would say, 'they were besties.'"

"That town is right on the border. Most people have family on both sides of the fence."

"It's certainly true of Cal Phillips. He has relatives in both countries on his mother's side. Her maiden name is Herrera."

"Any chance she's related to the man they call Dueño?"

"There's no immediate connection that I can find, but it's possible he's a distant relative. I'm still mapping out all the possibilities. All I know about Dueño so far is that he's big over there. And well protected. I'm not just talk-ing about his men. Government officials won't give up any information on him, either. There's no paperwork on him. It's almost as if the guy doesn't exist."

Went without saying the man had help. "Except we both know he does. What are we going to do to stop him?"

"I have guys working round-the-clock to uncover the

location of his compound, but it's risky to mention his name. Just knowing he exists is enough to get a bullet through the skull. My investigators have to move slowly on this one."

Reed didn't have a lot of time. "I'll involve my brothers' agencies. See if we can move any faster that way."

"We need all the help we can get on this. I'll let you know as soon as I hear anything else."

"I appreciate it. What about Knox? Where is he now? Should be easy enough to detain him for questioning. Maybe we can get answers out of him."

"I'd like nothing more than to have that SOB in custody. Only problem is, he's gone missing."

Damn. "You think he's lying low or permanently off the grid?"

"Could be either. Or dead. The minute I started asking questions about him in connection to Dueño put his life in danger. If Dueño's inner circle didn't get to Knox, then government officials might. They'll do anything to cover their tracks."

Reed didn't like any of this new information. It meant that Emily might never be safe. And now that he was knee-deep in mud with her, they could be digging two graves. He informed his boss about the upcoming summit.

"I have a guy who's been able to climb fairly high in Delgado's organization. I'll see if he can get information for us."

"Sounds good. Keep me posted."

"Be careful out there. I don't want to visit you in the hospital again. Or worse."

"I have people I can trust watching my back this time. But I won't take anything for granted."

Reed ended the call.

"Did I hear that right? This is related to what happened to you before?" Luke clenched his back teeth.

"Yeah. It's the same group." Reed had every intention of locating that compound and finding a way in.

"I can take some time off work. The FBI will understand. Nick will want to be involved, too."

Normally, Reed would argue against it. He knew better than to turn down an offer for help when the odds were stacked this high against him. "Okay."

"I know what you're thinking. Don't be stupid," Luke warned.

"No, you don't."

Emily stretched and yawned. "Don't be stupid about what?"

"Nothing," Reed lied. His brother knew Reed had every intention of locating that compound and doing whatever it took to breach it.

Because anger boiled through his veins that the same son of a bitch who'd gotten to him wanted to hurt Emily.

Chapter Twelve

Reed opened his eyes the second the truck door opened. He glanced at the clock on the dashboard. He'd caught an hour of sleep.

"Relax, just filling the tank. You need anything from inside?" Luke asked, motioning toward the building.

"I'm good. Thanks."

Emily was already awake, sitting ramrod straight. The sober look on her face said Luke had filled her in. Reed hoped she hadn't overhead their conversation, especially the part where his brother was pressing about her. Reed might not've come across the right way, and he didn't want to jeopardize whatever was going on between them by a misunderstanding. He almost laughed out loud. What *was* going on between them? If someone could fill him in, then they'd both know.

All he knew was the thought of spending more time with her appealed to him. He actually *wanted* to talk to her, and he wasn't much for long conversations otherwise. And the way her body had fit his when they were lying in bed last night was as close to heaven as this cowboy had ever been.

And yet, there was a lot he didn't know about her, and her family.

He made a mental note to talk to her about what he'd said to Luke when the two of them were alone again, which a part of him hoped would be soon. Based on the look on her face, she'd heard something, and he hated that he'd hurt her.

The chance to bring up the subject came when Luke finally quit fidgeting in the backseat and shut the door to pump gas. Thankfully, the large tank would give Reed a few uninterrupted minutes.

"Did my brother tell you about the conversations I had with our older brother and my boss?"

She nodded, keeping her gaze trained out the opposite window.

He couldn't read her expression from his vantage point but knew it wasn't good that she couldn't look him in the face anymore. Bringing up what he really wanted to talk about was tricky, so he took the easy way out. "Did you get any rest?"

Did he really just ask that? Reed was even worse at this than he'd expected to be. Most of the time, he sat back and observed life. That was his nature. He'd never been much of a "wear his feelings on his sleeve" kind of person. This was hard.

If he'd blinked, he'd have missed her second nod.

This was going well. Like hell.

"Emily, would you mind looking at me?"

Slowly, she brought her face around until he could see the tears brimming in her eyes.

"Did I say something to hurt you?" Stupid question. Of course he had.

"No." A tear got loose and streaked her cheek.

He reached up and thumbed it away, half expecting her to slap his hand. She didn't. So, he took that as a good sign and forged another step ahead. "My brother was asking questions I wasn't prepared to answer about us."

"Is there an 'us,' Reed?" Her lip quivered when she said his name.

"It's too soon to tell. If we met under different circumstances, there's no doubt I'd want to ask you out. We'd take our time and get to know each other. Figure it out as we went, like normal people. Start by dating and see where it went from there."

"But now?"

"Everything feels like it's on steroids. Plus, to be honest, I'm not looking to be in anything serious right now. I'm not ready to make a change in my career."

"Why would you have to change jobs? It's only dating, right?" The bite to her tone said he'd struck a nerve.

Damn. Trying to make things better was only making it worse.

Luke had finished pumping gas and disappeared inside the store. He'd be back any second, and Reed would never be able to dig himself out of this hole in time if he didn't do something drastic. Did she need to know how he felt about her? Since he was no good with words, he figured showing her was his best course of action.

Gently, slowly, he placed his hand around Emily's neck and guided her lips to his. That she didn't resist told him he hadn't completely screwed things up between them. Besides, he'd been wanting—check that—he'd been needing to kiss her again the whole damn day.

And that was confusing until his lips met hers and, for a split second, he felt as if he was right where he belonged. Did she feel the same? A sprig of doubt had him thinking she might slap him or push him away.

Instead, she deepened the kiss. With all the restraint

he had inside, he held steady, ever mindful of not hurting her. Control wasn't normally something he battled.
With Emily, he had to fight it on every level, mind and
body. Let emotions rule and he'd want to get lost with
her. His body craved to bury himself in the sweet vee of
her legs. With those runner's thighs wrapped around his
midsection, he had no doubt he'd find home.

But that wouldn't be fair to her.

He had nothing to offer. He wasn't ready to leave his
profession behind, and a woman like Emily deserved
more.

She pulled back first. "Who said I was looking for a
serious relationship? I have my career to think about, and
that takes up most of my time."

Reed was stunned silent. She'd pulled the "my work
comes first" card? Okay. He needed to slow down for
a minute and think. "Where do you see yourself in the
future?"

"Independent."

What did that mean? From what he'd seen of her so
far, she was too stubborn to let men with guns scare her.
Reed respected her for it. Did she mean alone? She'd also
just turned the tables on him. "Why can't you have a job
and a boyfriend?"

"That what you're asking for?"

"What if I was?"

She stared impassively at him. "I don't do relationships, so I'm not asking for one with you if that's the
impression you're under."

Wait a damn minute. "Why not? Is there something
wrong with me?"

"Not that I can see. I don't have time. I work a lot of
hours. If I haven't lost my job, I plan to throw myself

back into my work when this whole ordeal is over." Her expression was dead serious.

"And what if I wanted to see you sometime?"

"I live in Plano. You live south…somewhere…I'm not exactly sure where."

"I live in a suburb of Houston. Rapid Rock."

"At least that's one thing I know about you." She paused, and a weary look overtook her once bright eyes. "How far away is that from Plano?"

"Three hours. Four if traffic's bad."

"See. Too far."

"People date long distance, you know. It wouldn't be the end of the world."

"I don't."

Luke opened the door, and reclaimed his seat before shutting the door.

The conversation stalled. No way was he finishing this with his brother in the vehicle. Reed was butchering it all by himself. He didn't need an audience to tell him what he already knew. He was bad at relationships.

"Your brother and I spoke about federal protection," she said stiffly.

That's what this was all about? Had Luke encouraged her to go into WitSec? Why did Reed feel betrayed?

"And? What did you decide?"

"I want to discuss my options with your older brother."

"Fine."

THAT ONE WORD was loaded with so much hurt, an invisible band tightened around Emily's chest. She didn't want to upset Reed, but what else could she say? The truth was that she might need to go into the program, just as Luke had suggested. His thoughts made perfect sense, and she'd be a fool to put herself or Reed in further danger.

Besides, Reed was determined to bring the man who'd shot him to justice. And she couldn't blame him. If the shoe were on the other foot, she wouldn't rest until the person was behind bars, either.

And Dueño? That was a man who needed to be locked up forever along with a pair of former Border Patrol agents.

She'd talked to Reed about work, but the reality was she most likely would have to get a new identity if she wanted to live, let alone have a family of her own some-day, which was what she wanted. Wasn't it?

The idea had held little appeal after her last relation-ship. She'd all but closed herself off to the possibility of a real life, or a family of her own. Being with Reed stirred those feelings again, and she couldn't ignore them with him around. Not that he'd be there for long.

The minute he went after Dueño, she feared Reed would be hurt. If she showed up to visit him in the hos-pital, she'd be dead. From the looks of it so far, she'd be running the rest of her life. And the worst part was she'd almost be willing to risk everything for a man like Reed.

How crazy was that?

Especially when he'd made it seem as if he didn't share the same feelings. She'd overheard his conversation with his brother earlier. Her chest had deflated knowing he didn't feel the same way she did.

Which was what exactly?

Were her feelings for Reed real? Could they last? How could anyone figure out anything with bullets flying and cars exploding?

Maybe it would be best to separate emotions from

logic in the coming days in order to stay alive. They could figure out the rest later.

That she felt Reed's presence next to her, bigger than life, wouldn't make it easy as long as they were around each other. But difficult was something Emily had a lot of experience with. And challenging relationships were her specialty.

"We heading to my place?"

"It seems safe enough to stop in and let you grab a few of your things." Reed looked at her intensely before turning his head to stare out the window. A storm brewed behind those brilliant brown eyes. "We'll have to be careful, though."

"That would be nice. I'd love to wear my own clothes again. Can't even imagine what it would feel like to have my own makeup."

"After we make a pit stop, we'll head to my gran's ranch outside in Creek Bend."

Luke cleared his throat. "It'll be easier to connect with Nick and talk about options there."

The tension between brothers heated the air for the rest of the ride.

Emily was grateful to step outside and stretch her legs when they arrived.

Luke had parked a block away, explaining that he wanted to walk the perimeter before they approached her town house. Seemed like a good idea to her. Not to Reed. He grumbled at pretty much everything his brother had said, and she knew it had to do with him talking to her about federal protection.

She wasn't sure what she wanted to do. The promise of a clean slate offered by the program wasn't the worst thing she could think of at the moment. But then, what about her mother?

The woman barely hung on as it was. What would she do if the only daughter she could depend on disappeared altogether? Emily was the only one holding the family together. And she barely did that. Heck, she didn't even know where a couple of her siblings had disappeared to in the past few years. As soon as they'd reached legal age, they'd bolted and hadn't looked back. Emily most likely would've done the same thing, except that she remembered what her mother had been like before. She'd had the same fragile smile, but it had been filled with love.

And now? Everything in Emily's life was unraveling.

She took a deep breath and stepped out of the truck. The thought of having a few comforts from home gave Emily's somber mood a much-needed lift. It was amazing how the little things became so important in times of disaster. Something such as having her own toothbrush and toothpaste put a smile on her face.

Once Luke gave the all-clear sign, she and Reed moved to her town house. She packed an overnight bag as the men watched the front and back doors.

Reed's oldest brother had done a great job patching the hole he'd put in her window. The board should hold nicely until she could get a glass person out next week. Next week? Those few comforts had relaxed her brain a little too much. Clean pajamas wouldn't take away the dangers lurking or give her back her life.

Just to be sure no one could steal her pass codes, she pulled them out from underneath her desk where they were taped and tucked them inside her spare purse. Luckily, she'd taken only her driver's license, passport and one credit card to Mexico. Everything else had been tucked into an extra handbag she kept in the closet.

She checked her messages. The resort had called concerned that she hadn't been back to her room since Tuesday. She made a mental note to reach out to the manager and have her things shipped back to the States. Everything wasn't a total loss. She'd get her IDs and credit card back.

Except if she took up the offer for federal protection, she wouldn't need any of those things again, would she?

Her pulse kicked up a notch. No amount of deep breathing could halt the panic tightening her chest at the thought of leaving everything behind. She prayed it wouldn't come to that.

For now, she was safe with Reed and Luke. She'd have to cross the other bridge when she came to it. Surely, the right answer would come to her. As it was, she was torn between both options.

A good night of sleep might make it easier to think. No good decision was ever made while she was hungry and tired.

She took one last look around her place—the only place that had felt like home since she was a little girl—and walked downstairs. "I'm ready to go."

Reed stood at the window, transfixed.

"Everything okay?"

"They must've been watching for you. Someone's coming. Go get my brother. Tell him we have company."

Chapter Thirteen

Reed crouched behind the sofa near the window as his brother entered the room. "I saw two men heading this way."

"The back is clear," Luke said, standing at the door.

"Then take her out that way." Reed's weapon was drawn and aimed at the front. Anyone who walked through the door wouldn't make it far. He had no intention of being shot and left for dead again.

"I'm not leaving you." The finality in Luke's tone wasn't a good sign.

Reed needed his brother to get Emily to safety. "They get her and it's game over. And I might never be able to find Phillips. Get her out of here, and I'll meet you at the truck in ten minutes. I need to make these guys talk."

Luke hesitated. "I'm not sure that's a good—"

"Go. I'll be right there. If you don't leave now, it'll be too late."

His brother stared for a moment then helped Emily out the back. Good. Last thing Reed needed was someone getting to her. He had no doubt that he and Luke could handle whatever walked through that door, but Emily was weak from her injuries, and Reed didn't want to take any chances when it came to her. Besides, he'd already hurt her enough for one day.

Crouched low, he leaned forward on the balls of his feet, ready to pounce.

The doorknob turned. Clicked.

A loud crack sounded, and the door flew open. These guys were bold. Didn't mind walking through the front door or making noise to do it. Also meant they were probably armed to the hilt.

"Stop right there, and get those hands in the air where I can see them. I'm a federal agent." Reed paused a beat and peered from the top of the sofa. "I said get those hands in the air where I can see them."

The first bullet pinged past his ear as the men split up.

Reed fired a warning shot and retreated into the kitchen. The sofa wouldn't exactly stop a bullet.

His boot barely hit tile when the next shots fired, *ta-ta-ta-ta*.

Reed leveled his Glock and fired as bullets pinged around him. Hit, the Hispanic male kept coming a few steps until his brain registered he'd been gravely wounded. Blood poured from his chest, and he put his right hand on it, trying to block the sieve.

As Reed wheeled around toward the back door, a second man entered. Reed was close enough to knock the weapon out of the taller Hispanic's hand. Tall Guy caught Reed's hand and twisted his arm.

Instead of resisting, Reed twisted, using the force of a spin to gain momentum until he broke Tall Guy's grasp. Reed pivoted, losing his grip on his gun in the process, and thrust his knee into Tall Guy's crotch. He folded forward with a grunt.

About that time, he must've seen his partner because

he let out a wild scream and threw a thundering punch at Reed's midsection, then grabbed his shoulders and pushed until he was pinned against the granite-topped island.

Reed's first thought was that he prayed these guys didn't bring reinforcements. His second was that he hoped like hell Emily and Luke had made it to the truck. With Emily's injuries, Luke wouldn't be able to take care of her and fight off several men. It wouldn't be possible. Not even with his gun, although Reed knew his brother would do whatever he had to in order to protect Emily.

Another blow followed by blunt force to the gut and Reed dropped to his knees, the wind knocked out of him. He battled for oxygen as he pushed up, trying to get back to his feet. His gun was too far to reach. Tall Guy must not've seen it slide across the room and under the counter.

Reed, fighting against the hands pushing him down, reared up and punched Tall Guy so hard his nose split open. Blood spurted.

That's when he saw the glint of light hitting metal. The sharp blade of a kitchen knife stabbed down at him. Reed shoved Tall Guy, ducked and rolled to the left. The knife missed Reed's head a second before it made contact with the tile.

What Reed needed was to restore the balance of power. And he could do that only on his feet.

Tall Guy dived at Reed, landing on top of him. Even though Reed rolled, Tall Guy caught Reed on his side. The knife came down again, fast.

Reed rolled again, catching Tall Guy's arm. The knife stopped two inches from Reed's face. Testing every muscle in his arm, Reed held the knife at bay. Another roll and Reed might be able to reach his Glock. With a heave, he managed to roll and stretch his hand close enough to get to his gun.

He fired and fought Tall Guy. Problem with shooting a guy was that it still took a few moments for his brain to catch up. Reed struggled against the knife being thrust at him for the third time.

The tip ripped his shirt at his chest. Blood oozed all over Reed.

As if the guy finally realized he was shot, he relaxed his grip on the knife. It dropped, clanking against the tile.

Reed couldn't afford to wait for more men to show. He pushed Tall Guy off and managed to get to his feet. His boot slicked across the bloody floor. He wobbled, and then regained his balance, stepping lightly in the river of blood. Before he left, he fished out his cell and took a picture of each man.

All he could think about was Emily's safety. He broke into a full run as soon as he closed her back door.

Maybe Luke could get the FBI to clean up the mess Reed had left behind. As soon as he knew Emily was safe, he'd blast the pictures of his attackers to all the agencies and see if he got a hit.

His heart hammered his ribs. Not knowing if she was okay twisted his gut in knots.

Rounding the corner, he pushed his burning legs until the outline of the truck came into view. Where was she? Where was Luke?

He didn't slow down until he neared the empty vehicle. Sirens already sounded in the distance. If Luke had made it out safely, surely he would've called one of his contacts. Or had a neighbor heard gunfire and called the police?

His heart pounded at a frantic pitch now as he surveyed the area, looking for any signs of Emily and Luke, or worse yet, indications of a struggle.

Was the truck locked?

He moved to the driver's side and tried the door. It opened. That couldn't be a good sign.

The town house-lined street was quiet, still.

Motion caught the corner of his eye.

"Get in the truck," Luke shouted.

A shotgun blasted.

"Get inside and get down." Luke carried Emily in a dead run. By the time he reached the truck, sweat dripped down his face. He tossed Reed the keys.

Reed hopped into the driver's side and cranked the ignition, thankful the two people who mattered to him most right now were safe. The truck started on the first try.

Luke hauled Emily inside and hopped in behind her. He pulled an AR-15 from the backseat. "Drive."

"Buckle up." Reed stomped the gas pedal. He didn't want to admit how relieved he was to see that Emily was okay. He didn't want to consider the possibility anything could happen to her. Exactly the reason he needed to talk her into WitSec. That might be the only way to keep her safe.

"Bastards brought reinforcements. I couldn't get to you in time," Luke said, in between gasps of air.

"You should've kept Emily in the truck."

"And let them kill you? They had three more on the way."

"I could handle myself." He kept his gaze trained out the front window, but he could see from his peripheral that Emily was assessing his injuries. "I got cut with a knife. Most of this blood belongs to someone else."

"Oh, thank God." She let out a deep breath. "I thought…"

He took her hand—it was shaking—and squeezed. "I'm okay."

"Cut right and we'll lose them," Luke said. "They're on foot."

Reed brought his hand back to the wheel and turned. "They must've been watching to see if she'd show up since they didn't find the pass codes."

Luke picked up his cell phone, studied it and held it out. "We're done dealing with these jerks on our own. I'll call in the guys."

No way would Reed refuse the help. Dueño was closing in and Reed still had no idea who the guy really was or in which region of Mexico he lived. Not to mention he remembered what both of his brothers had gone through in the past couple of years. A determined criminal was a bad thing to have on his radar.

"I have a few pics we need to circulate." He fished out his cell and handed it to his brother.

"Good. We can blast these out to all federal agencies."

"Gil's number is on the log. Make sure he gets copies."

"Will do, baby bro." Luke made a move to set the phone down. It pinged. "Looks like we got a hit already."

Reed tightened his grip on the steering wheel.

Luke studied the screen. "Both of these guys are wanted for trafficking. One's name is Antonio Herrera."

"Looks like we found our family connection. That's Cal's mother's last name."

"Tell me about it." Luke cursed. "We have an ID on the other one, too. Name's Carlos Ruiz."

"Guess I don't know him."

It took a little extra time to reach Gran's place in traffic, but Reed couldn't think of a better sight than Creek Bend as the ranch-style house came into view.

In order to protect them and the ranch, men had been stationed along the road and Luke had been reassured there'd be more in the brush, as well. He'd had to call ahead to let Gran know in case she spotted one and panicked. She'd been prepped on what to expect upon their arrival, too. Mainly, so she wouldn't be surprised when she saw Emily's condition. Even though she was improving, she still had the bumps and bruises to prove she'd been through the ringer. Seeing it was another story altogether.

Potholes had been filled on the gravel road, making for an easy trip up the drive. Good that Emily wouldn't be bounced around. The last time she repositioned in her seat, she'd sucked in a burst of air, and her arm came across her ribs. She'd caught herself and immediately sat up.

The fact she'd been silent for the journey didn't reassure Reed. Eyes forward, she hadn't slighted a glance toward him. He needed to make things right. But first, she needed to heal.

The front door flew open before they'd even made it out of the truck.

Nick and Sadie rushed out first, followed by Gran, their sister Lucy, and Julie.

The tension in Reed's neck eased a notch. There was something about having Emily here at the ranch with his family that made sense in this mixed-up world.

Reed offered his arm for Emily to use as leverage to get out of the truck. She sat there, stone-faced.

Damn that he couldn't tell what she was thinking. Did the whole clan overwhelm her?

He hoped not. He hoped she could get used to them being around.

She took his arm, but as soon as she raised hers, she flinched.

"You're hurting worse than you want to let on, aren't you?"

"I'm sure I'll be better after a little more rest."

Why did she always have to armor up when he got close? Reed had never met someone so strong on the outside. Or someone who'd erected an almost impenetrable fort on the inside.

The pain medication she'd been given at the hospital had worn off. "The nurse gave me a few pills. I'll bring them to you as soon as you get settled."

His sister and sister-in-law took over with Emily, and he was left standing, holding the door open.

Nick waited for the women to take Emily inside before he motioned for Luke and Reed to stay out.

"I've got men everywhere. No way can anyone get through the woods or down that lane unnoticed. Now, I know you want to go after these guys, and we will. All three agencies have men on this."

"Good. We'll need all the help we can get." Reed shuffled his boots on the pavement. Dueño's men were smart. If there was a way inside the ranch, they'd find it. But with all the agencies sending men, it would be a lot harder.

"In the meantime, we wait for good intel," Nick said. "Oh, and Gran lifted the ban on guns in the house. Said she figured rules had to be bent when it made sense. She's still on me for not warning her beforehand when I brought Sadie there to protect her."

Reed thanked his brothers. They bear-hugged before splitting up. "Luke here has some news for her."

"Gran already saw Julie wearing a wedding ring." Nick glanced from Reed to Luke.

"And?" The way his face twisted up Reed would think his brother was waiting to hear about another serial killer on the loose.

"You know Gran. There were hugs and tears."

Luke blew out his breath. "Thank heaven for small miracles."

"You're another story, I'm afraid."

"In the hot seat?"

"Guess you didn't see the way she looked at you when you first pulled up."

"I'm hoping Emily will keep Gran distracted and this one can slide past," Luke joked.

It was nice to laugh with his brothers. Maybe Reed should take Luke up on his offer to start a PI business together when this whole mess cleared up. And it would get straightened out. Reed had the chance to right two wrongs in this case. He had no other thought but to bring justice to the men who'd hurt Emily and put his life in danger. Five minutes alone with the bastard and a shallow grave would suit Reed better at this point, but he'd settle for a life behind bars.

"Good luck with that. She might give Julie a break, but you're a different story," Reed teased.

"Yeah. As long as she doesn't bring out the switch, I'll be okay." Luke cracked a smile.

"We knew she'd never really use it on us, but the threat of it was a powerful tool. Even if she had, it wouldn't have hurt more than letting her down."

"We could be trouble," Nick added.

"And we still are," Reed agreed.

"I better go face the music. Get this over with," Luke conceded.

"Better you than me, dude," Reed gibed.

"Where's my backup when I need it?"

"Nick here is your man. I'm planning to take a look and see what needs to be done in the barn. Been sitting too long and need to stretch my legs." Not ready to go inside, he headed to the barn instead.

There was nothing like hard work to clear his mind— a mind that kept circling back to the woman inside. Because having her at Gran's felt more natural than it should.

Chapter Fourteen

When all the outside chores were done and the sun kissed the horizon, Reed took off his hat and walked inside.

Concentrating on work when Emily was in the house took far more effort than he'd expected. The need to check on her almost won out a dozen times. He wanted to be with her, and especially right now, but that's about as far as he'd allowed his thoughts to wander.

Gran stood in the kitchen. "I fixed biscuits and sausage gravy. Your favorites. You want a plate?"

"No, ma'am. I'm not hungry yet. Thank you, though. I'll make those disappear later," he said with a wink. "How's Luke?"

"He's resting. She is, too. In case you were wondering," Gran said, returning the gesture.

Not her, too. Luke had already read him the riot act about Emily. Reed didn't need to hear it from Gran, too. "If anyone needs me, I'll be out checking the perimeter. I'll ask the men on duty if they want any biscuits."

"Here. Take this with you. I already packed sandwiches for them." She motioned toward a box on the table.

Reed kissed her on top of the head before hoisting the box on his shoulder, and grimaced. "Keep mine warm."

He wouldn't eat before he made sure the men outside had food.

Gran opened the door and Reed nodded as he left for the barn. He pulled out a four-wheeler and loaded the box of food on it, using a spring to hold it on the back.

Riding the fence took another half hour. It was dark by the time Reed returned the four-wheeler to the barn and moved inside again. He showered and ate before heading down the hall to Emily's room.

Standing at the door, he listened for any signs she was awake. He hated to disturb her if she was asleep.

Instead of knocking, he cracked the door open and waited. The need to see her, to make sure she was okay, overrode his caution about entering a sleeping woman's room.

Warning bells sounded off in his head all right. And not the ones he'd expected. These screamed of falling for someone he barely knew. Reed prided himself on his logical approach to life. He'd always been the one to watch and wait. Emily made him want to act on things he shouldn't, against his better judgment. Exactly the reason he didn't get all wound up when it came to feelings. Then again, he'd never met someone who'd made him want to before, not even his fiancée. Had he pushed her away? Not given her a reason to stay? The obvious answer was yes. Reed was realistic. Even so, when it came to Emily, he needed to force caution to the surface.

"Hi." Her voice was sleepy and soft.

Reed was in trouble all right. He sat on the edge of the bed and touched her flushed cheek with the backs of his fingers. "How are you, sweetheart?"

"Ibuprofen does a world of good." She moved back to give him more room, froze and flinched.

"Don't hurt yourself."

"I'm okay." She inched over and patted the bed.

"Can I ask you a question?" he asked softly.

"Sure." There was plenty of light in the room. Enough to see her beautiful hazel eyes.

"Why do you always have to put up such a brave front?"

"I don't."

"Honesty. Remember? We promised not to lie to each other."

Her lips pressed together and her face was unreadable. "I just don't know how to be another way."

What did she mean by that?

Tears welled in her eyes.

"Why not?"

"Because it's always been me being the strong one. I don't expect you to understand. You have all this family around, helping, ready to lay their lives on the line for you." She paused and her shoulders racked as she released a sob. "I have me."

Reed couldn't begin to imagine how lonely that must feel. "Can I ask what happened to your parents?"

"Doesn't matter. It was a long time ago."

"It does to me."

"Why?"

"I want to know more about you. It'll help me figure out how to help you." Why couldn't he tell her that he wanted to know more for reasons he didn't want to explore? What was so hard about telling her he might be falling for her? Maybe it would break down some of that facade she so often wore.

Then again, move too fast and she might scurry up a tree like a frightened squirrel. She deserved to know how he felt about her. And he had every plan to tell her as soon as he figured it out himself. Right now, he didn't need the complication.

But that still didn't stop him from reaching out and touching her. He moved his finger across her swollen lip, lightly, so he wouldn't hurt her.

Those big hazel eyes of hers looked into his. "When my father left, my mother was devastated."

"Did he leave before or after he found out she was sick?" Reed's fists clenched. He knew exactly how it felt to have a father walk away. Except that Reed had had so much love in his life, it didn't affect him as much as it had his brothers.

"I wasn't completely honest with you before. I was too ashamed. She isn't sick in the traditional sense."

"Alcohol?" Lots of people turned to the bottle in hard times. Not everyone had the strength to battle their demons.

"No. Not exactly." She looked away.

"You can tell me anything. I won't judge you for it."

"How could you not? You have this big family around you, supporting you. I don't even know where to start."

He cupped her face and turned it until she was looking at him again. "Right here. Right now. This is where you start. Tell me what happened."

Tears fell and she released a sob that nearly broke Reed's heart. "It's okay. I'm right here."

She buried herself in his chest. "She drank at first. On a date with a man she barely knew, she was raped. After that, she just lost it. She joined a religious cult and moved us to California. Then she started popping out babies. She said that the men at the House cared about her, at least. Everything was up-front and honest. No one lied to her."

"At least there were people around to help. Your mother must've needed that."

"Except that they didn't. I did the best I could raising them. I'm used to living alone, being alone. Helping everyone else. But, it's not entirely her fault. I think she's sick or something. Underneath it all, my mother is very sweet. I mean, I know everything she did sounds bad, but she loved me. She kept me with her. Not like my father, who just walked away after pretending to care for us."

And Emily never wanted to be that vulnerable. It was starting to make sense why her work was so important to her. "It's okay to love your mother. Sounds like she was all you had growing up."

"It's screwed up, though, right?"

"Not really. I mean, all families are messed up in some way."

"She tried when I was little, but after all that, my mother was just…lost."

Also explained why Emily didn't want to be dependent on a man.

More sobs broke through, even though she was already struggling to contain them.

"It's okay to cry, sweetheart."

A few more tears fell that she quickly swiped away. "I just can't afford to let my guard down."

"Crying doesn't make you weak. But holding all that in for too long will break you down from the inside out one day. You don't have to put up a brave front all the time."

"I can't afford to fall apart. I'm all I've got."

"Right now, I'm here. Let me take some of the burden." Sure, Reed's father turned out to be a class-A disappointment, but he'd been one person. Reed couldn't imagine what it would feel like if everyone in his life had let him down.

"You are so lucky to have all this. To have such an amazing family…this beautiful ranch."

"We're a close-knit bunch. But then, we've always had to be. What about you and your father? He left your mother, but did he ever contact you?"

"I found him once. It was the week before college graduation. An internet search gave me his phone number, address. I thought I'd hit the jackpot. Guess as a child I'd convinced myself that even though he left Mom, he still loved me. I decided that he must not have known where I was after we moved. And that's why he never called on my birthday or had me to his house for Christmas."

"Kids make up fantasies when one of their parents is gone."

"Did you?"

"I didn't need a father. I had two older brothers constantly looking out for me. The whole situation was harder on them, and especially Nick being the oldest. He stepped inside a father's shoes and filled them out. I was damn lucky to have him."

"That must've been hard on your mother, too."

"She's an amazing woman for taking care of us the way she did."

"Did you ever look for your father?"

"Guess I never felt the need to find the man with all these jokers around trying to tell me what to do." He tried to lighten the mood, and was grateful when she smiled even though it didn't last.

"Some of my younger siblings were sent to live with other relatives when people found out about what went on at the House."

Reed had heard stories, too. Read reports about places like those, none specifically about the place where she grew up, but there were others. He'd had to raid a few since some on the border were known to harbor criminals. All kinds of marginalized people lived there. The thought Emily had endured a place like that made his heart fist in his chest.

Her bottom lip quivered.

He leaned forward and pressed a light kiss to her mouth. He kept his lips within an inch of hers. Her breath smelled like the peppermint toothpaste Gran kept on hand. "You're one of the bravest people I've ever met to go through all this alone and still be this normal."

She blinked. He imagined it was a defensive move to hold back more tears from flowing.

"Thank you, but—"

He pressed his lips to hers again to stop her from speaking. Her fingers came up and tunneled into his hair.

She pulled back and kept her gaze trained to his. "I'm not sure if throwing myself into my work or at you makes me brave, but I appreciate what you're saying."

"You survived. You carved out a normal life. You did that. And with no one there to support you. You are an amazing woman. And I'm one lucky bastard."

This time she pulled his lips to hers, deepening the kiss.

That moment was the second most intimate of his life. And both had to do with Emily. Both had similar effects on his body. He was growing rock hard again. No way would he risk hurting her. Both made him want to get lost in her.

She needed sleep, not complications.

"Think you can get some rest? I can come back to check on you in the morning."

She opened the covers. "Stay with me tonight?"

All his alarm bells warned him not to climb into those covers with this beautiful and strong woman. The more he learned about her, the more he respected her courage, her strength.

He thought about the women he'd dated in the past, and not one measured up. Not even the one he'd intended to marry.

Reed slipped under the sheets and took to his back.

Emily curled around his left side and he wrapped his arm around her. The perfect fit.

"Fair warning. You get any closer, and I can't be held responsible for my actions. Keep in mind the other bedrooms are at the opposite end of the house."

A laugh rolled up from her throat. It was low and sexy. "That makes two of us."

Getting stiff when Emily was around wasn't the problem. He had no doubt the sex would blow his mind. But then where would that leave them after?

Why should he risk getting closer to her when he knew the second he found Dueño's location and arrested him, their professional need to be together would be over?

With enough people working on the case, the information could take a little time to track down, but they'd find it…find him.

Emily deserved to have her life back. And, just maybe, she'd find a little room for him in her day-to-day life, too.

"GOOD MORNING," REED SAID as he brought a fresh cup of coffee to Emily. He'd made it a habit in the couple of weeks she'd been staying in Creek Bend.

She pushed up and then rubbed her eyes.

"You want me to come back later?"

"No. I'm awake. Besides, you brought coffee. That just about makes you my favorite person right now."

"Then I won't keep you waiting." He handed her the cup, smiling.

"You're up early. Any news?"

"We have three government agencies with men on this case and no new information. They've interviewed everyone linked to Knox and Phillips. Nothing there. All our hopes were riding on the summit, and that turned out to be a disappointment. Luke said one of his contacts in the FBI thinks he might be getting close to a breakthrough."

"It's only been two weeks."

Reed glanced at the clock. "Your boss will expect you online soon."

"Thanks for helping me figure out how to handle this whole mess with Jared. I'm still surprised he didn't want to come see me personally at the hospital to make sure I wasn't lying. But then, I've never heard him so worried."

Her boss was being a little too concerned, which didn't sit well.

"The part about you being in a wreck is true. We just fudged the rest." The only good news that had come out of the past couple of weeks was that Emily was up and moving. Her injuries were healing nicely. The bruises on her face were gone, and she was even more beautiful than before. Reed could see her light brown hair starting to show through, and he could only imagine how much more beautiful she'd look when it was restored to its natural color.

However, being landlocked was about to drive Reed to

drink. Plus, he was getting used to waking up to Emily every morning. A dangerous side effect.

"Caffeine and ibuprofen are my two best friends right now." She hesitated. "Aside from you."

"Good to know I rate right up there with your favorite drugs," he teased. "Speaking of which, I have a couple right here."

"I don't know if I've said this nearly enough, but thank you." Her playful expression turned serious as she took the pills from his outstretched hand. "Seriously, I don't know what I would've done without you."

The band that had been squeezing his chest for the past two weeks eased. Warmth and light flooded him. How had she become so important to him in such a short time? And maybe the better question was: what did he plan to do about it? "I have a feeling you would have figured out a way to get through this on your own."

And he already knew the answer to his question. He didn't plan to do anything about it. Their lives were in limbo until he found Dueño and put him behind bars.

"I'm not so sure." She tugged at his arm, pulling him toward her.

Happy to oblige, he leaned in for a kiss. The taste of coffee lingered on her lips. "Keep that up and I won't let you out of bed."

"Promises, promises."

"You let me know when I wouldn't be hurting you and I have every intention of living up to that promise."

They both knew sex wasn't an option while she was healing. They'd pushed it a time or two with bad results. He wouldn't take another risk of hurting her until he could be sure.

Reed chuckled. Restraint wasn't normally a problem

for him, but with Emily his normal rules of engagement had been obliterated. Holding back had become damn painful, especially when her warm body fit his so well.

"What? Why are you laughing?"

"No reason. You just focus on getting better. We'll take the rest one step at a time." Going slow would be better for the both of them. They both crashed into this—whatever *this* was—like a motorcycle into a barricade. They hit a brick wall wearing nothing but jeans and a T-shirt. No helmet. No protective gear. Being forced to cool their heels wasn't the worst thing that could happen as his heart careened out of control.

Reed Campbell didn't do out of control.

The pull toward Emily was stronger than anything he'd felt for Leslie, and he'd almost made the grave mistake of spending the rest of his life with her. Thinking back, had he even really wanted to marry Leslie? Or had the idea just seemed logical at the time?

They'd been dating for two years. She'd dropped every hint she possibly could they were ready. Even then, Reed had been cautious.

When she'd given him the ultimatum to move their relationship forward or she'd walk, he'd thought about it logically and decided to take the next step. She had a point. They'd been together long enough. She'd moved in, even though he hadn't remembered asking her to. Slowly, more and more of her stuff had ended up at his place. First, the toothbrush and makeup appeared in his bathroom. She'd been sleeping over a lot, so he figured it made sense. Then, she left a few clothes in his closet. Again, given the amount of time she spent at his place, a logical move.

When she'd approached him with the idea they could

both save money if she didn't renew her apartment lease, he'd thought about it and agreed. He'd gotten used to Leslie being there. Didn't especially want her to leave. So, he figured that was proof enough he must want her to be there. He didn't think much about it when she spent Saturdays watching shows about wedding dresses. Or when she'd started asking his opinion about what she'd called "way in the future" wedding locations. Bridal magazines had stacked fairly high on the bar between the living room and kitchen when she finally forced his hand.

Reed knew he wasn't ready for marriage. He figured most men who'd come from his background would have a hard time popping that question of their own free will.

When he'd really thought about it, he decided that he might never be ready. But it had made sense to marry the person he'd spent the past two years with, so he'd asked.

With Leslie, he didn't have to stress out about picking a ring because she'd already torn out a picture of what she wanted from one of those bridal magazines and left it in his work bag the day before.

She'd thought of everything.

Had he really ever been crazy in love with Leslie?

Being with Emily was totally different.

Sitting there now, enjoying a cup of coffee with her, gave him a contented feeling he'd never known. And made him want to jump in the water, feetfirst, consequences be damned.

And it was most likely because they couldn't, but he'd never wanted to have sex with a woman as badly as with her, either.

If absence made the heart grow fonder, then abstinence made a certain body part grow stiffer. Painfully stiff.

"I better hit the shower." And make it a very cold one at that.

"You sure I can't convince you to climb under the covers where it's warm?"

He stood and shook his head. The naked image of her just made him certain he'd need to dial the cold up even more.

Besides, he was going stir-crazy being holed up at the ranch for two solid weeks. He itched to get out today, figuring he'd be fine on a motorcycle.

Reed kissed Emily's forehead, ignoring the tug at his heart, and then strolled to the shower to cool his jets. And a few other body parts, too.

Drying afterward, he slipped on boxers, a pair of jeans and T-shirt. He didn't stop to eat breakfast, heading out the back door while everyone was busy instead.

He grabbed a helmet and pulled his motorcycle out of the barn. Anyone watching the house wouldn't know who was leaving since he and his brothers looked alike from a distance. Plus, he knew a back way off the land and onto the street.

The men watching were used to Reed checking the perimeter every morning by now, so he kept his helmet tied to the back so they could see it was him.

Before he hit the main road, he stopped long enough to slip on the helmet. A pair of shades would disguise him further.

On the road, he expected to feel free.

He slipped past the inconspicuous car parked behind an oak tree. There were two others he spotted and, most likely, one or two he didn't. The Feds were keeping an eye on movement outside the ranch. Since no laws were being broken, there wasn't much they could do about Dueño's men being there.

Getting out proved easier than he'd expected. Then again, they wanted her, not him. It would be clear to anyone that he was a man.

Winding around the roads, pushing the engine, should feed his need for adrenaline and feeling of being out of control while completely in control. The speed, the knowledge that he could go faster than anything on the road with him, made it almost feel as if he became one with the bike and was in total control. Gran had always said that Reed had a need for controlled chaos, which was a lot like how he felt with Emily. Instead, the more distance he put between himself and the ranch gave him an uneasy feeling in the pit of his stomach and an ache in his chest.

What if Dueño's men made a move while Reed was gone and they were one man down? Reed might have unwittingly just played right into their hands. Logic told him it didn't matter. The ranch had almost as much coverage as the president. Even so, being away from Emily left him with an unsettled feeling.

Reed needed to turn around and get back to the ranch. Except when he did, he noticed two cars heading toward him in the distance. They were coming fast, side by side on a two-lane road. Isolating him was the best way to get rid of him.

Run the other way and they'd chase him. The farther he got from the ranch, the more vulnerable he became.

Reed clenched his back teeth and opened the throttle. Looked as if he was about to be forced into a game of chicken.

Chapter Fifteen

Since Reed had left, Emily had a hard time concentrating. She'd eaten and logged on for work. An uneasy feeling had consumed her when she saw him take off on his motorcycle.

Being here with his family had brought a strange sense of rightness to her world.

Maybe it was just the thought of family that made her all warm and fuzzy on the inside. With a deserter for a dad and a sweet-but-lost mom, Emily had never known a life like this.

And how adorable was Gran?

No doubt, she was the one in charge of these grown men.

The house itself was well kept and had a feeling of ordered chaos. The rooms were cozy, and keepsakes were everywhere.

Emily dressed, ate and stepped outside. Life abounded. A small vegetable garden was next to the raised beds of planted herbs. Flowers grew in pots on the back porch complete with a couple of chairs around a fire pit. Birds nested in the trees.

But her favorite place was the barn and being with the horses.

No wonder the Campbell boys had grown up to be caring men. A place like this would do that.

After two weeks of big family meals, great conversation and being with people who genuinely cared about each other, Emily was surprised at how much this place felt like home to her.

And yet, it was like a home that had existed only in her imagination before. How many nights as a child had she fantasized her life could be more like this?

Hers had been filled with dry cereal and people who talked a whole lot about love without it ever feeling sincere.

Love, to Emily, was making a real breakfast for others. Love was kissing good-night and being tucked into bed. Love was being brought coffee in the morning.

Reed?

Did she love Reed?

Would she even know love if it smacked her in the forehead?

Emily hadn't known this kind of love existed. It was fairy tales and happily-ever-after. She had no idea it could happen in the real world. Even when she'd dated Jack, she hadn't felt like this. She had needed her space, and that's most likely why he'd been able to get away with being married while he told her she was the only one.

She cursed herself for not recognizing the signs. He hadn't worn a wedding ring. There was no tan line on his left hand.

But then, he hadn't had to be very deceiving when she let him come around only once a week and had insisted he go home every night.

Guess she was an easy target.

Then there was the guy she'd dated before him, who

after six months had told her three was a crowd in a relationship. She thought he was accusing her of seeing someone else. When she told him she wasn't, he laughed bitterly and said he knew she wasn't seeing another man. He was talking about her job.

Being with Reed was different. It felt completely normal to wake up in his arms every day.

And that thought scared the hell out of her.

REED AIMED DEAD center at the car on his left. A split second before his wheel made contact with the bumper, he swerved to the center line, narrowly avoiding both cars.

If that wasn't enough to kick his heart rate into full speed, a near miss with a shell casing was. The blast had come from behind.

Soon, the cars would turn around, but they'd have a hell of a time trying to catch him. The curvy road would make him a harder target to see and, therefore, shoot.

Getting back inside the ranch would be tricky. If he could get a message to Luke, he could alert the men.

Reed had to take a chance and stop. He pulled over and eased his motorcycle into the brush for cover.

The text that came back clued Reed in to just how pissed off his brother was. In retrospect, his brother was right. Going for a ride this morning was a boneheaded move.

Not two minutes later, a pickup truck roared to a stop followed by two unmarked vehicles.

Reed expected a lecture when Luke hopped out of the driver's seat.

"You take the truck. I'll bring in the motorcycle." His brother had been too focused on the mission of bringing Reed home safely.

He understood. There was no room for feelings during an op.

Reed nodded and thanked Luke before taking a seat behind the wheel. Knowing that he came from a place of love humbled Reed. After spending time with Emily and hearing about her childhood and lack of family, he'd grown to appreciate his even more.

As he wound down the twisty road home, he thought about what it must've been like for her. To grow up surrounded by so many people in a communal house, but so very alone at the same time.

He hoped having her at the ranch had helped her see real families, though not perfect, existed. For his, Gran had provided the foundation. She'd given them a roof over their heads when their father had taken off.

Reed's mother was one of the strongest people he knew, but bringing up five kids alone was a lot for anyone. He wished Emily had had a mother who sacrificed for her the way his mother had for them. Her life wasn't about date nights or spa appointments. She'd given hers to her children. And yet, she didn't resent them. Loving them seemed to feed a place inside her soul and make her even stronger.

Emily was strong, too. And his chest puffed with pride every time he thought of her, of what she'd survived. Yeah, she had bruises. But hers were on the inside, and even with them she'd opened her heart a little to him.

Pulling up the drive, seeing her leave the barn stirred a deep place inside him. A spot deeply embedded in his heart that was normally reserved for people with the last name Campbell.

His circle might be small, but the relationships in it weren't. And they had a name. He needed to remind himself that Emily's last name was Baker. Leslie had pretty much destroyed the chance of anyone else finding their way inside permanently when he'd caught her in bed with Cal.

When he'd been shot later that day, she hadn't visited him in the hospital. For the week he'd been ordered on bed rest, she'd stopped by all of once.

The moment he'd broken consciousness, he'd waited for her. For an excuse. For an apology. Something.

She'd texted him that she was moving out of their apartment. Said that he wasn't there for her in the way Cal had been. Reed wondered if Cal was still there for her. If they were together somewhere in the hot, unforgiving jungle. It would serve her right.

Reed parked the truck as Emily came toward him.

"I thought you left on a motorcycle."

"That was a bad idea."

Luke didn't speak when he passed them. Reed understood why. They didn't need words to know his brother was frustrated. Inside the perimeter, the ranch had sufficient protection to keep out a militia. Reed was angry with himself. No one could punish him for his mistakes more than he could. Wasn't that exactly what he'd been doing since Leslie?

Not letting another woman get close to him?

Emily reached for his hand. "Come on. I want to show you something in the barn."

He had some explaining to do when Luke cooled off. In the meantime, staying out of his way wasn't such a bad idea. "What did you find in there?"

"Come on. You'll see." She tugged at his hand.

With her palm touching his, he could feel her pulse, her racing heartbeat. "Fine. But shouldn't you be working?"

"I'm on lunch break. Besides, Jared called. Said he didn't like me trying to work so much while I'm trying to heal."

Reed would bet her boss was concerned for more than just her general well-being. Was he just a little too worried? "I'll bet he is."

"Said he wanted to come see me."

A bolt of anger split through Reed's chest, spreading to his limbs. Logic said she wasn't interested in the guy. So, where was reasoning at a time like this? As it was, Reed's brain didn't seem to care a hill of beans about being rational with his body pulsing from anger and something else when she was this close—something far more primal.

He pushed those thoughts aside. "So what did you want to show me in the barn?" A few things came to mind. Her naked topped the list. So much for leaving those high-school-boy hormones behind. Her being vulnerable, with him putting her in that position, must be weighing on his mind and his body was trying to compensate. Otherwise, if those pink lips curled one more time he'd have no choice but to cover her mouth with his and show her just how much of a problem she was creating for his control.

Once again, his logical mind had failed.

Thinking back, didn't most of his ex-girlfriends accuse him of thinking too much in their relationships?

And now Emily had come along and seemed to be doing her darnedest to turn everything that made sense to him upside down.

And he didn't like one bit that her boss seemed to want more than nine-to-five from her. He'd ask Nick to run a background check on the guy just to see what

Reed was dealing with. "I don't think you ever told me Jared's last name."

"Why do you need it?" she teased.

"I like to know everything I can about my competition," he teased.

"Sanchez. His name is Jared Sanchez."

"Has he always kept such a tight leash on his employees? Or just you?"

"He's the worst. I can't go to the bathroom at work without him knowing my schedule."

Reed remembered his conversation with Jared. The man had acted as if he was guessing where she'd gone on vacation. A background check sounded like a better idea all the time. "So, what did you end up telling Mr. Sanchez?"

"That I was resting at a friend's place, and it was too far for him to drive."

Reed would've felt better if she'd said she was at her boyfriend's. "Feel free to use me as an excuse. I don't mind."

"What? And tell him we're in a relationship?" She snorted. "The only people you'll ever really trust have the last name Campbell."

It wasn't that funny.

She stopped at the closed barn doors and covered his eyes with her free hand. "No peeking."

In the dark with his eyes shut, he resigned himself to be surprised and let her lead him inside.

"Don't open yet." She closed the barn door.

Even at midday, it would be fairly dark inside unless she'd turned on the lights.

"Okay."

She hadn't. He glanced around. Nothing looked out

of place. No big surprises lurked anywhere. "Yep, it's a barn."

"Uh-huh."

"What did you want me to see exactly?"

She steeled herself with a deep breath, pushed up on her tiptoes and kissed him.

His arms around her waist felt like the most natural thing to him. He splayed his hand low on her back, springing to life more than a deep need to be inside her.

Her hands came around his neck, her body flush with his, and his body immediately took over—his hands moved down to her sweet bottom and caressed.

The little mewling sound that sprang from her lips heightened his anticipation.

The kiss ended far too fast for his liking. She looked him deep in the eye.

"You can't break me." She took his hand again, smiled a sexy little smile that caused his heart to stutter, and led him upstairs to the loft.

A thick blanket had been spread on the floor. There was a soft glow lighting the room by one of those battery-powered lamps.

Logic told him to turn around and walk out before he couldn't.

Practical thinking said he shouldn't let his relationship with a witness be muddied by sex. Even though he had no doubt it would be mind-blowing sex.

Reasoning said as soon as this case was over he'd be back in South Texas and her life would continue in Plano.

All of which made sense. Not to mention he'd be breaking agency rules.

Reed knew he should say something to stop her. If things ended badly between them, it could jeopardize his career, his future with the agency and his future employability.

"I wanted to show you this." Emily stopped in the center of the room, locked gazes and slowly unbuttoned her shirt.

One peek of that lacy pink bra did him in. To hell with logic.

He crossed to her before the blouse hit the floor.

This close, he could see hunger in her eyes that he was certain matched his own. His lips came down hard on hers, claiming her mouth, as his tongue thrust inside searching for her sweet honey.

The sound she released was pure pleasure.

He cupped her breast and then pressed his erection to her midsection, rocking his hips. "You sure about this?"

She nibbled his bottom lip. "I've never been more certain about anything in my life."

Emily took a step away from him and shimmied out of her jeans. He almost lost it right there when he saw her matching panties. Pink was his new favorite color.

Her hands went to the button fly of his jeans, but his made it there first. He toed off his boots, and his jeans hit the floor shortly after. She'd already made a move for his T-shirt, so he helped the rest of the way. "That's better. We've both had on way too many clothes."

Her musical laugh, a deep sexy note, urged him to continue.

Looking at her, her soft curves and full breasts, her gaze intent on his, was perfection. She was perfection. "You're beautiful."

That she blushed made her even sexier.

"Nothing hurts, right?" he asked, needing reassurance. This time he was already lost in her, and stopping would take heroic effort. He hoped like hell he'd be up to the challenge if he needed to be because looking at her in the low lamplight was the most erotic moment of his life.

"Fine. You first, then." He guided her onto the blanket, watching for any signs of pain.

There were none, so he made his next move. Her panties needed to go. If she could handle him pleasuring her with his tongue, he could think about filling her with something else.

He started at her feet and peppered kisses up the insides of her calves, her thighs.

Placing his hands gently on her silken thighs, he slowly opened her legs, checking to make sure she didn't grimace. Nope, he was good to go.

Her uneven breathing spiked as he bent down to roll his tongue on the inside of her thigh, moving closer to her sweet heat.

Using his finger, he delved inside her. A guttural groan released when he felt how hot and wet she was for him. His tongue couldn't get there fast enough. He needed to taste her. Now.

Her hands tunneled into his hair.

There were no signs of pain, just the low mewling of pleasure intensifying as he increased pressure, rubbing, pulsing his tongue inside her as she moved her hips with him.

Using his thumb, he moved in circles on her mound, and his tongue delved deeply, moving with her, tasting her, until her body quivered and she gasped and then fell apart around him.

He shouldn't be this satisfied with himself. He couldn't help it. Pleasuring her made another list he didn't know he had until meeting Emily. This one involved his favorite moments.

Taking a spot next to her, giving her a chance to catch her breath, he couldn't hold back a smile.

"That was… You are…amazing." She managed to get out in between breaths.

He turned on his side, needing to see her beautiful face. The compliment sure didn't hurt his ego. Truth was he wanted to hear her scream his name. And only his name.

Setting the thought aside when she rolled over to face him and gripped his straining erection, he took a second to really look at her. Perfection. She was that rare combination of beauty and strength. He wanted to bury himself inside her and get lost. Her mouth found his and he took the first step on the journey to bliss.

His heart hammered against his ribs, and for a split second he was nervous about his performance. He opened his eyes and chuckled against her lips. The vibration trailed down his neck, through his chest and arms.

Hers did the same. She smiled, too.

And his heart took a nosedive. He was in trouble, which had nothing to do with how great the sex was about to be.

Careful not to put too much weight on her, he rolled until he was on top of her. Her legs twined around his hips.

"Hold on." He tried not to move much while he wrangled a condom out of his wallet, grateful his jeans were within arm's reach. He ripped it open with his mouth, his hand shaking as he rolled it over the tip.

"Let me help with that." Her touch was firm but gentle

as she rolled the condom down his shaft, lighting a fire trail coursing through his body, electrifying him.

When she gripped him and guided him inside her, he nearly exploded. His body shook with anticipation as he eased deeper.

"You won't hurt me." Her gravelly voice was pure sex.

Reed needed to think about something else if he wanted this to last. And he did. Until her hips bucked, forcing him to let go of control and get lost in the moment, the sensation of her around him, her innermost muscles tightening around his erection.

Looking into those gorgeous hazel eyes, he thrust deeper, needing to reach her core.

There was no hint of pain, only need.

They moved in a rhythm that belonged only to them. He battled his own release until she shattered around him, begging him not to stop. She breathed his name as she exploded, her muscles tightening and contracting.

When her spasms slowed, he pumped faster and harder until his own sweet release pulsed through him.

Exhausted, he pulled out and disposed of the condom before collapsing beside her.

"That was amazing," she said.

"Yeah. We're pretty damn good together, aren't we?"

"Best sex of my life."

"I couldn't argue that." His, too. He hauled her close to him.

She settled into the crook of his arm.

"And you're okay?"

"Never felt better."

"You tired? You want to go back to bed and rest?"

"I want to go back to bed all right. But not to rest." Her smile lit up her eyes.

He could get used to looking into those eyes every day. His erection had already resurrected. "Good. Because I'm going to need to do that a lot more to you today."

She reached for his wallet, which was still splayed on the floor, and retrieved another condom.

He didn't need to worry about whether or not he would be able to accommodate her. He was already stiff again. "I want this, too. Believe me. But should we wait a little while?"

"Still worried about hurting me?" She opened the package and rolled the condom down his shaft.

"I'm always going to want to protect you. But, yeah, I don't want to cause you any pain. You've been through enough and you're just now healing."

"Then, cowboy, you better lie back and let me show you what I can and can't do." She mounted him, still wet, and he groaned as she eased onto him.

"Better watch out. I could get used to this."

The corners of her mouth tugged when she bent down to kiss him. "Good. Because I'm counting on it."

Chapter Sixteen

After taking a break from work to get fresh air, Emily walked into a house full of Campbells, and one very special little bundle in one of the women's arms. Reed introduced her to his sister Meg and her husband, Riley, the proud parents of baby Hitch.

"His name is Henry, but we call him Hitch for the way he 'hitched' a ride into our hearts," Reed explained.

Emily's heart skipped a beat at the proud twinkle in his eyes when he looked at the baby. And a place deep inside her stirred. She wanted a baby someday. But now? She'd kept herself so busy with work, it had been easy to avoid thinking about it. Maybe she'd been afraid to want something that seemed so far out of reach, something she had no idea how to attain given her screwed-up past. Seriously, her mom lived as if it were the sixties, probably a throwback to her youth. Although Emily could appreciate the Beatles, she believed the present was far more interesting than the past. And yet, hadn't she been stuck there in some ways, too?

Meg leaned toward Emily, who couldn't help but smile at the baby. "Do you want to hold him?"

"I would like that very much." Emily sat in a chair and

took the sweet boy, who was bundled in a blue blanket with a brown horse stitched on it. "I love this."

"Gran made it." Meg beamed and Emily figured the look of pride had more to do with Hitch than his wrap.

"It's beautiful. And he's a gorgeous baby."

Emily expected to be overwhelmed by the group, but everyone stood around and chatted easily. Their level of comfort with each other was contagious. Instead of wanting to blend in with the wallpaper, as she usually did in groups of people she barely knew, she enjoyed joining in conversation. Laughing. There was real laughter and connection, and love.

Reed stood next to her, smiling down during breaks in bantering with his brothers, and her heart skipped a beat every time.

When was the last time she was so at ease in a room full of strangers? Heck, in any room?

Emily couldn't remember if she'd ever felt this relaxed, normal, as if she belonged. She credited it to the Campbells' easy and inclusive nature. They had enough love for each other, and everyone else around them. Images of Christmas mornings spent huddled around a tree in this room came to mind. Warmth and happiness blanketed her like a summer sunrise.

Hot cocoa and a blazing fire in the fireplace would be more than enough heat to keep them warm as they exchanged gifts.

There'd be laughter and Reed by her side. The realization Emily wanted all those things startled her. Because she was a guest there. And no matter how comfortable they made her feel, she didn't belong. Had never belonged anywhere or to anyone.

The thought sat heavy on her chest as she cradled the baby closer, trying to edge out the pain.

She glanced at the clock. It was time to set her fantasies aside and retreat to her room to work.

Glancing down at the sweet, sleeping baby, the earth shifted underneath her feet. Good thing she was already sitting or she feared she'd lose her balance. Because holding this little Campbell was nice. Better than nice. Amazing. And Emily could only imagine how much more fantastic it would be to hold her own child someday. One created with the man she loved.

Realization hit her in a thunderclap, ringing in her ears. She did want to have a baby. *Someday.*

For now, she had more pressing needs. To stay alive, for one. To keep her job, for another. Maybe once she got back on her feet, she'd be in a position to open herself up to other possibilities, as well.

"I better get back to work." She stood and reluctantly handed the little bundle over to his mother. "Thank you for letting me hold him. He's a sweet baby, and it was gracious of him not to cry." The only babies she'd ever held before had wailed. Of course, she'd been stiff as a board when their mothers had placed them in her arms. The babies most likely picked up on her emotions. And now she realized she'd also been afraid—afraid that by holding them, she'd realize she wanted one of her own. Maybe, when her life was straight and she met the right man, she'd be ready to think about a future.

Meg rewarded Emily with a genuine smile. "He's especially good when he's sleeping, which isn't much these days since he started teething."

Reed followed her into her room, took off his shoes and made himself comfortable on top of the bedspread.

Seeing him there, fingers linked behind his head, made her almost wish she could start on her future now.

Silly idea.

But then great sex had a way of clouding judgment. And theirs had been beyond anything she'd ever experienced before. She couldn't help but crack a smile. Until reality dawned and she realized her time in paradise had a limit.

As soon as the right call came in, Reed would be out of there, tracking the most deadly man in Mexico. If this was anyone else other than Reed, she'd consider going into WitSec and asking him to come with her. She knew in her heart a man like him wouldn't give up his family or go into hiding for the rest of his life. He was honest, strong and capable. Injustice would hit him harder than a nail. And he wouldn't sleep until he'd made it right.

Her worry was probably written all over her face, but she couldn't help it. She'd grown to care for Reed in the past few weeks, and she didn't want to think about him leaving. She'd also overheard conversations where she knew they were getting close to pinpointing a location.

"What's wrong?" His dark brow lifted.

"Nothing. I was just thinking how cute Hitch is," she lied.

He patted the bed next to him. "Come here."

She sat on folded knees, facing him.

"I can't help if I don't know what's really bothering you. Is it my family? They can be a bit much for people when they're all together."

"Not at all. I like being with them very much."

He leaned forward and kissed her. "That's nice because they love you."

She couldn't hold back her smile. Love? Being near

Reed had a way of calming all her fears. But the last thing she needed to do was learn to depend on him. His family might love her, but did he?

"What is it really?" He kissed her again. "I hope you know you can tell me anything."

Except the part where she'd lost the battle against the slippery slope and was falling for him. Hard.

She had no doubt Reed could solve any problem, aside from that one.

"I'm just thinking about a work issue. It's nothing."

"WHY DON'T I believe that?" Reed surprised himself at just how important Emily had become to him in the past couple of weeks.

She leaned forward and kissed him.

"Keep that up and we're not leaving this room for a long time," he teased, but he was only half joking.

"Who said I'd mind?" She laughed against his lips.

Before she could get too comfortable with that thought, he flipped her onto her back and pressed his midsection into the open vee of her legs. "I have no problem rallying for that cause."

Reed cursed as he heard his name being called from down the hall. "Ignore it."

"Not happening, cowboy. Not in broad daylight with your family in the next room shouting for you."

"I was afraid you'd say that. Hold that thought. I'll get rid of them and be right back." He kissed her again and then hauled himself out of the bed. He sat on the edge for a long moment, needing to get control over his body before he headed out of the room. "This is your fault, you know."

"What did I do?"

"Made it where I can't get enough of you."

Luke shouted again.

With a sharp sigh, Reed pushed off the bed and headed down the hall. He followed the voice to the kitchen, where Nick and Luke were seated at the table. They were staring intently at someone's laptop.

"What did you guys find?"

"Turns out that name you wanted us to check out the other day is involved," Nick said.

"Jared Sanchez?"

"Yeah. His mother's maiden name is Ruiz."

Reed cursed and fisted his hands. So much of Jared's behavior made sense now. No wonder he'd been so forgiving. He was keeping tabs on Emily. "So, he's related to the guy at the town house."

"That's not all. He's up to his eyeballs involved," Luke said.

"I'll kill that SOB myself," Reed ground out. "What else did you find?"

"Sent in a couple of boys to 'talk' to him and once he started, they couldn't shut him up. Turns out his cousin— your friend from the town house—realized what a cash cow Jared could be with his job at SourceCon."

Reed's jaw twitched. He didn't like where this conversation was going. "Go on."

"Jared swears he didn't want Emily to get hurt. Says he made his cousin promise nothing would happen to her. Jared's the one who gave up her location at the resort. She was supposed to be returned once she gave the codes. No harm. No foul. Jared wouldn't be connected to the crime and he'd make sure she kept her job."

"Except she didn't have her passwords."

"With her access to accounts in major banking institutions, Dueño must've also realized the kind of money on the line because he doesn't normally get personally involved. When she wouldn't give him what he wanted... well...you know what happened next."

Anger burned a raging fire inside Reed. "Tell me Sanchez is in a cell."

"Of course," Nick said quickly. "And there's a silver lining. Ruiz feared for his life when the job went sour and turned state's evidence. He gave up the location of Dueño's compound. We had it checked out and our guys confirmed it. Dueño's compound is in Sierra Madre del Sur, midway between Acapulco and Santa Cruz."

"And they're sure it's him?"

"Ninety-six percent certainty." Luke repositioned his laptop so Reed could see the screen. "That's our guy."

"Dueño?"

"That's him."

Reed took a minute to study the dark features and black eyes. "I need a plane."

"You need to check your messages. Your boss wants you to stand down on this one," Luke said.

"No way. I'm not letting someone else risk their lives for this."

"That's exactly what we thought you'd say. We stalled your boss. A chopper's on its way to take us to the airport."

"What do you mean *us*?"

"We're going with you."

"It's too dangerous."

The look on both of his brothers' faces would've stopped anyone else dead in their tracks. But Reed was immune. "Look, I'm not saying you're not the best at what you do, but you have families now. I can't let you take that risk for me."

"What the hell is it with you and families?" Nick asked, disgusted. "I know how to do my job."

Reed wouldn't argue the point.

"And if my baby brother is going anywhere near that compound, I'm going with him. This isn't just your fight. They messed with a Campbell. We stand together."

"Goes without saying."

"Then stop being a jerk and let us help you," Nick said flatly.

Luke added, "I don't trust anyone else to watch your back."

Reed couldn't argue that point, either. He felt the exact same way. "Okay, then. Whose resources are we using for this? Because it doesn't sound like my boss is going to pony up."

Luke raised his hand. "FBI wants this guy, so they said they'd back the mission. However, anything goes wrong, and we're on our own to explain it. We can do whatever we want with the jerk who shot you if we find him. He's a bonus."

"Or collateral damage," Nick interjected.

"I'd like to see him spend a long time behind bars. Dying is too easy for him." Reed paused and then clapped his hands together. "Sounds like a party. So when do we leave?"

"About half an hour. We'll get close to the suspected location and then wait it out until the middle of the night."

"Sounds like you have it all figured out." Reed needed to tell Emily about the plan. He felt a lot better about his odds with his brothers backing him. "What coverage do we have here in Creek Bend?"

"Enough to ensure the safety of a dignitary in a red zone. When this is over, we have to talk about setting up our own company. Just us brothers," Luke said, but the deep set to his eyes said he wasn't joking around this time.

Reed glanced at Nick. "What do you think about the idea of us going into business together?"

"After what happened to me, heck, I'm the one who suggested it."

"Did not," Luke interrupted. "You know this was my original idea from way back."

Reed smiled. Working with his brothers wasn't a half-bad idea. His job at Border Patrol had gone sour the day he'd realized he couldn't trust some of his own. As it turned out, his shooting wasn't as uncommon as it should be. But then, one should be enough. "First things first. Let's go pick up a couple of hot tamales across the border, and then we'll talk business."

He couldn't ignore the possibility that forming an agency with his brothers would bring him back to North Texas and closer to Emily. Would she be open to exploring the idea of them as a couple when he returned? For now, he had to figure out a way to tell her he was about to leave. For a split second, he considered taking her with him. Having her by his side was the only way he could be certain she'd be safe. But bringing her to Dueño's door wasn't a bright idea. There were enough federal men crawling through Creek Bend and around the ranch to keep an eye on her and his family.

The right way to tell her he was leaving didn't come to him on his walk down the hall. He stopped at her doorway and asked if he could enter.

One look at his serious expression and her smile faded,

disappearing faster than a deer in the woods at the scent of man.

"What did your brother say?"

He kissed her, mostly to reassure himself, because he suddenly wasn't sure how she'd react to the news.

Tension bunched the muscles in his shoulders worse than a Dallas traffic jam as he prepared himself for the worst.

When she realized how dangerous his job was, she might not want to see him anymore. Especially once he gave her back her life, which he had every intention of doing by morning. He also had every intention of living to see it…but he couldn't make promises on that one.

The right words to tell her still eluded him, so he just came out with it. "We found him."

Reed studied her expression, surprised at how much he needed her reassurance. But she was completely unreadable. Should he tell her about her boss? On second thought, maybe he should wait. He could explain everything once this ordeal was over.

"When do you leave?"

"Soon. A chopper's on its way."

She drew in a deep breath. "And you're sure it's him?"

"You can never be one hundred percent, but this is about as close as it gets." He took her hand, relieved she didn't draw away from him.

Staring at the wall, as if she was reading a book, she took another deep breath. "Okay. We should get you ready to go."

She wasn't upset? No begging him to stay? "You're all right with this?"

"'This' is what you do, right?" Her honest hazel eyes were so clear he could almost see right through them.

"Yeah. It is." No way could she be okay.

"And 'this' is what you love. It's part of who you are, right?" There was no hesitation in her voice.

Was it possible she understood? "Yes."

"I'm falling hard for you, Reed Campbell. I wouldn't change a thing about you." She smiled, leaned forward and kissed him. "Who am I to complain about your job?"

Did she really mean that? He studied her for a long moment then squeezed her hand. He didn't like the idea of leaving her, especially since Dueño's men were never far. The best way to protect her was by putting Dueño in jail. "You are someone who has become very special to me."

"Good. Because I happen to like who you are, Mr. Campbell. You're kind of dangerous." She peppered a kiss on his lower lip. "And mysterious."

She captured his mouth this time then pulled back just enough to speak. "And I happen to think that's very hot."

Chapter Seventeen

Reed gathered his pack, loaded it onto the chopper and climbed aboard. The loud *whop, whop, whop* couldn't drown out the sweet sound of Emily's last words. It was still foreign to him that someone could become so special in such a short amount of time. His feelings defied logic, which confused the hell out of him. And he didn't need to be thinking about it when he should be focused on his mission.

To make this day more complicated, he didn't like being away from her, or not being there to protect her. Even though the ranch was under lockdown by the FBI.

Finding and arresting Dueño was the best way to keep his family safe. Throw in the bonus of possibly locating the man who'd betrayed Reed, and he'd be doubling down on this mission.

No matter what happened, Reed would be ready. He and his brothers had gone over the operation's details a half dozen times at the kitchen table. Reed had memorized the map. No one needed to be reminded that although the FBI funded the detail, it wasn't sanctioned by the US government. Meaning, if things went sour, they'd be on their own.

But he and his brothers would be in constant communication. Plus, they had the added bonus of knowing each other inside out. Most teams trained for years to get that kind of chemistry.

The chopper took them to DFW airport, where they climbed aboard a cargo plane that would take them to Oaxaca, Mexico.

All joking stopped during the three-hour flight the moment they crossed the border into Mexico. From there, they'd board a smaller aircraft headed to a military airstrip in the foothills of Sierra Madre del Sur, and it'd be a quick half-hour drive from there.

Flights had left on time and they were on schedule as the second plane landed. Every mission had its quiet time so that the men could gather their thoughts.

They were all business as they met the driver. He'd take them to the base of the mountains then leave. They'd be on foot for the rest of the journey.

From the airport to camp took another half hour. The camp had been set up at the base of the mountains. It wasn't much more than a tent and the makings for a fire. There was wood and a circle of rocks. Since both Nick and Reed had learned the hard way that not everyone could be trusted, Reed suggested they relocate as soon as the driver returned to his vehicle.

His brothers nodded.

As soon as the vintage Jeep disappeared, Reed pulled up the tent stakes. "I say we camp an hour from the compound at the most."

"Good idea," Nick said.

They'd walked a mile in silence when Luke finally spoke up. "She'll be all right, you know."

"I hope."

"They couldn't protect her any better than if she'd been placed in WitSec," Luke continued.

That Reed didn't know the men she was with personally didn't sit well on his chest. Especially after what Nick had gone through a year ago when a US marshal supervisor had gone bad. Reed knew all about working with the unpredictable as a Border Patrol agent. All it took for a dozen bad seeds to be planted was a piece of legislation mandating his agency double up on personnel in order to stem the flow of illegals. Reed didn't mind the legislation; the idea was in the right place. But mandating all the hires happen in a month wasn't realistic. Detailed background checks took longer than that to execute and return.

The current system made it way too easy for criminals to make it into the system as agents. His grip tightened around his pack. Phillips and Knox were prime examples.

But it was rare for a US marshal to turn.

"I hope you're right." Being separated made him jumpy. Fine if it kept him that much more alert while on his mission. Not so good if it distracted him. "How do you guys deal with it?"

"What?" Luke asked.

"The job. Having someone back home."

"I know what Leslie did, but it should never have been that way," Luke said. "Julie has never asked me to quit my job."

Nick rocked his head back and forth in agreement. "Sadie, either. Why? You think Leslie had a point?"

When Reed really thought about it, no. He didn't think she had a valid point. He'd been on the job when they met, so she knew what she was getting into from the get-go. "I can't blame her for not wanting to sign on to this."

"Then she shouldn't have from the beginning," Luke said emphatically as he eased through the brush.

"There should be a clearing with a water source over this next hill," Reed said, changing the subject. "We can camp there."

"I think I can speak for Nick when I say being in a relationship in this job is a good thing as long as it's with the right woman." Luke wasn't ready to let it go.

"How so?" Reed knew all about being in relationships with the wrong ones.

Luke didn't hesitate. "Training gives you the skill set to handle any mission. A family gives you the mental edge to make sure you make it out alive. I have so much more to come home to now. I can only imagine what it'll be like when we have kids."

There was something different about Luke's voice when he said the last word. If there was a pregnancy, his quickie wedding made more sense. "Do you have something else you want to tell us?"

"Yeah."

"And you waited until we were out in the jungle before giving us a hint?"

"If Gran freaked about the wedding, what will she say about this?"

"She'll be as happy for you as we are," Nick interjected.

The image of Emily holding Hitch edged into Reed's thoughts. Something deep and possessive overtook him at the memory. He shoved it away. Because it looked a little too right in his mind. And since he'd known her for all of two weeks, it didn't make any sense to start thinking about how beautiful she'd look pregnant with his child.

He climbed to the top of the hill and looked out at the lake in front of him. The ground was level enough to make a good campsite. "There it is. Let's settle down here for a few hours."

The climb to their new location had the added benefit of giving their bodies a chance to get used to the altitude. They would need to be at their absolute physical peak when they breached the compound later.

Every step closer to that complex and Reed's determination to put an end to all this craziness grew. Whether or not he spent another day with Emily, she deserved to have her life back. "Luke, you serious about starting an agency?"

His brother's surprised smile said it all. "Yeah. Why? You interested?"

"I might be." Options were a good thing, right?

Once this case was over and Cal was behind bars where he belonged, Reed could think about doing something else for a living.

"Then, let's talk about this tomorrow morning."

Reed knew what his brother was doing. It helped with nerves to start talking about the future. Knowing they'd have one gave the mind a mental boost. "Deal."

For the rest of this day, they'd settle around their camp and wait.

EMILY WRUNG HER hands as she paced. Focusing on work was a no-go. Reading a magazine didn't provide the distraction she needed. So, she resigned herself to worry.

What if something happened to Gran? It would be all Emily's fault.

And Reed? The thought of anything happening to him was worse than a knife through the chest.

With all the FBI crawling around, a cockroach couldn't slip past unseen. She wasn't worried about herself, anyway. Reed was the one running into danger, when most people ran the opposite direction.

He was brave and strong, and everything she admired in a man. It didn't hurt that he was drop-dead hotness under his Stetson.

The thought of anything happening to the man she loved seared her. *Love?*

Did she love Reed Campbell?

Oh, yeah, her heart said. And she figured there was no use arguing. The heart knew what it wanted, and hers wanted him.

Sleep was about as close as Christmas to the month of June. Hours had passed since her usual bedtime, but it didn't matter. Hot tea did little to calm her nerves. Warm milk had similar success.

She curled under the covers and tried to remember how she'd survived the many stresses of her childhood. Easy. She'd pictured her future exactly how she wanted it to be and then worked toward it with everything in her power. There was something incredibly powerful about making a decision and then holding it strong in her mind's eye.

Maybe she could use that same approach now.

It would be a heck of a lot better than wearing a hole in the carpet.

Determined to see his face again, she took a deep breath and pictured Reed holding Hitch at the family barbecue Gran had scheduled next month to celebrate Luke and Julie's marriage.

Closing her eyes tightly, she held that image in her mind as she drifted off to sleep.

THE AIR WAS still, the monkeys quiet.

Reed looked from one brother to another. "Give me a minute?"

They nodded and walked away, each in a separate direction. Apparently, he wasn't the only one with a ritual for when he intentionally put himself into harm's way.

This was the time he went into his private zone where he took a moment to think about his loved ones and re-committed himself to getting back to them safely. No way would he allow the only fathers he'd ever known, Nick and Luke, to be without their brother. Emily's face invaded his thoughts, too. He had every intention of see-ing her again…the way her face flushed pink with desire when he kissed her. The feel of her soft skin underneath his rough hands. Her strength under adversity. And her smile. Those were things to get home to.

Reed moved back to the edge of the lake. Anything happened and they had a place to stay the night. They could carry an injured man this far without too much effort.

Every mission had to have a backup plan. With only three of them on an unsanctioned assignment, they had only each other to depend on. There'd be no Blackhawk if this thing went south.

First Luke returned, then Nick.

Reed performed a final check of their emergency sup-plies, shouldered his pack and put on his night-vision gog-gles. His cell was on vibrate, but communication back home was pretty much dead for now.

The compound was an hour's hike. They'd given them-selves plenty of time to adjust to the altitude and hydrate for the trip. The mission had been timed to perfection. It was three o'clock in the morning. They'd reach the compound around four. They had roughly twenty minutes to locate the target and then drag his butt out of there.

A Jeep would pick them up at the original campsite at five thirty to take them to a waiting plane, which would be fueled and ready to go.

Dueño's actual place would be more difficult to reach. He'd built the small mansion in a valley that was flat, affording tall mountain views on all sides. Nature's perfect barrier. So, Reed would have to climb up and down to reach the place.

Based on intel, there were enough men with guns surrounding the nine-foot-high concrete fence to guard the president, all of whom were inside. Under the cover of night, Reed was confident they could make it down the side of the mountain undetected. Getting inside the gates would be a different story.

The hike was quiet, save for the soft steps behind him. Anyone else would have to strain to hear them. Reed could sense his brothers' movements. Years of playing in the trees long past dark on the ranch had honed their skills.

Luke was probably the most quiet of the trio. His military training had most likely kicked in at this point, and Reed hoped it didn't bring back bad memories.

At the peak of the last incline, a breeze carried voices from below. Reed made a mental note of how easily sounds traveled, and forged ahead.

The compound came into view as soon as he peaked. To say it was huge was an understatement. They'd seen it from a satellite picture, and yet the photo didn't do it justice.

Clearly, someone important lived here. A man like Dueño, someone with his power, would make his home in something like this. Crazy that a jerk like him made money hurting women.

The image of Emily when Reed had found her stamped his thoughts. She was beaten and vulnerable but not defeated. Dueño might have hurt her physically, but she'd made it clear that's all he could do.

From what Reed could see, coming in from the south, as they were, was still the best option. He'd wait for Luke's signal to continue.

Two thumbs-up, the sign to descend, came a minute later from Luke.

With each step down, Reed's temper flared. He'd become a master at controlling his emotions, and yet, getting closer to the man who'd hurt Emily, who had her running for her life, kept his mood just below boiling.

He'd enjoy hauling this guy's butt to the States, where he could be properly arrested.

Twenty more steps and they'd be at the concrete fence.

Luke popped over first. Then came the signal. Reed followed next, then Nick.

Crouched low, Reed moved behind the first guard.

With one quick jab, the guy was knocked unconscious. Reed pulled a rope from his bag and then tied and gagged the guy to his post just in case he woke before they'd finished.

They didn't have a lot of time.

It took another five minutes to locate the window of the room where the target was believed to be sleeping. A curtain blew in and out with the breeze. With all this security around, the guy didn't feel the need to close his windows. That was the first lucky thing Reed had encountered so far.

In his experience, a man got two, maybe three lucky

breaks on a mission. The op had to be planned to a T. Reed pulled on his face mask, giving the signal for the others to follow. When their masks were secure, he opened the tear gas canister and placed it on the sill. The gas wouldn't hurt anyone inside in case there were children, but it would disorient and confuse anyone who breathed it.

Reed pulled himself up and slipped inside. He rolled the canister toward the center of the room. Plumes of gray smoke expanded and filled the room. Before he could signal his brothers, a fist came out of nowhere. He took a hit to the face, dislodging his mask. He spun around and repositioned it. As soon as he got a visual on the guard, Reed kicked the guy. The blow was so hard, he took two steps back and began coughing as the gas shrouded him. He dropped to the floor and disappeared into the haze of smoke, giving Reed enough time to motion for his brothers to join him.

As they cleared the window, the light flipped on. The room was dense with smoke. Sounds of coughing were followed by footsteps.

Reed identified three distinct voices. Luckily, none belonged to children. He moved to the bed and handcuffed the biggest body. Luke had already dispatched the guard and Nick was subduing a screaming female.

When the guy spun around to face Reed, he got a good look at him. He released a string of curse words. This wasn't Dueño.

The door burst open and several men pushed through, choking and gagging as they breached the room. Reed studied their faces. Disappointment edged in when he realized neither Cal nor Knox was there.

Were they with Dueño? On their way to find Emily?

In fact, there wasn't nearly enough security at the compound. Had they mobilized most of their men to get to her?

Reed cleared the bed and yelled to Nick that the guy wasn't there. By the time they got to Luke, bullets were flying. Whoever was shooting couldn't see clearly, either. Not exactly the ideal scenario.

They needed to get out of there. Fast.

If Dueño wasn't here, he could be anywhere in Mexico, or Texas. And where was Cal? All hopes of finding him fizzled and died. An overwhelming urge to get back to Emily hit Reed faster than a car on the expressway.

"Abort!" he shouted, but his brothers were already to the window.

Fear gripped Reed. Had they just played right into Dueño's hands?

Chapter Eighteen

Emily jolted awake to the sound of glass being cut. Oh, God. She heard movement in the other room. She threw her covers off, hopped out of bed and grabbed the lamp on the bedside table. Her mind clicked through possibilities as she reached for her phone and shouted for help.

"Who's there? Somebody help." A shaky finger managed to touch the name of the supervisor she'd been given to call in an emergency on her phone.

Three men stormed her bedroom. Three guns pointed at her. Three voices shouted orders at her.

Adrenaline pumped through her. She could lie down and let them take her, or go out fighting. If she could stall long enough, maybe someone would hear her. She shouted again. Why wasn't he coming through that door?

Let the men with bandannas covering their faces take her and she might as well already be dead.

The first one rushed toward her, and the others followed suit. For a split second, she thought they looked like a bird formation. Emily reared back, grabbed the lamp and swung it toward the first man with everything inside her.

He took a hit hard enough for blood to spurt from his nose. Except the other two men were already there, grabbing her, before she could wind up and swing again. One jerked the lamp out of her hands.

The first man cursed bitterly, and she knew there'd be a consequence for her actions later. That didn't stop her from kicking another one in the groin. He bent forward but didn't loosen his grip.

With one man on each side of her and another behind, she was forced into the living room at the same time the front door burst open.

At least six men wearing vests marked SWAT surged inside the door, stopping the moment they saw the gun pointed at her temple.

"Stop or she's dead," one of the men said in broken English. "And we already took care of him."

The SWAT team didn't lower their weapons, but they didn't move, either.

A little piece of her heart wished it had been Reed storming through that door. Another broke for the officer they'd disposed of because of her. It would be too late because the men already had her. They'd torture and kill her once they got her to a secure location. But she wished she could see him one last time. She shut her eyes and tried to conjure up the details of his face, his intense and beautiful brown eyes. The sharp curve of his jaw. Hair so dark it was almost black.

If she concentrated, maybe his face would be the last thing she remembered.

Emily didn't open her eyes again until she was outside, being shoved toward a white van. By this time, officers were everywhere and she could imagine how helpless they felt. They'd sworn to protect, and the ones she'd met so far took that oath seriously.

It wasn't their fault. Not one had a shot with the way they'd used her as cover.

Dueño was powerful enough that if he got her to the border, it would be over. American law enforcement had no jurisdiction in Mexico. Without cooperation from the Mexican government, she'd be left defenseless.

Emily kicked the man in front of her. He spun around and smacked her so hard she thought her eyeball might pop out. Could she move out of the way enough for one of the SWAT officers to get a clean shot? It'd take more than that since one of the other two could shoot her.

No way would the officers risk her life.

Dread settled heavy on her shoulders as they forced her to move.

The van was only a few steps away, blocking the view of officers surrounding the ranch.

Let these men get her inside the vehicle... Game over. There'd be no cavalry.

She reared her right foot back again ready to deliver another blow, but it was caught this time. Twisting her body left to right like a washing machine, she struggled to break their grasps, to do anything that might give officers a line of sight to get off a shot and take down her captors.

The barrel of a gun pressed to her head. "Keep at it, bitch, and we'll shoot."

Why hadn't they already? Dueño must want her alive. She could only imagine the tortures he had planned for her. A shudder ran through her.

Even so, she'd pushed it as far as she could. Hopelessness pressed heavy on her chest as she was thrown into the back of the van. Her head slammed against the seat and something wet trickled down her forehead.

Pain roared through her body. Her injuries had been healing nicely until now. Being thrown around and kicked awakened her aches. But none of the physical pain was worse than the hole in her heart.

One of the men sat on top of her, his weight an anchor being tossed to the depths of the ocean.

"There. Now she won't move." His laugh was like fingers on a chalkboard, scraping down her spine.

He bounced, pressing her body against the seat so hard she thought her ribs might crack. She cried out in pain.

"Don't hurt her. Dueño wants her alive," the driver, a white man, said as he gunned the engine.

"I'm not killing her. But she deserves a little pain after breaking my nose." His words came out through gritted teeth, slow and laced with anger.

The emptiness of her life caused the first tears to roll down her cheeks as a stark realization hit her. She didn't fear death. She was only sorry for the life she'd led. Too many times she'd let her demons stop her from pushing herself out of her comfort zone. Her fear of ending up broke and needing some man to save her pushed her to spend too much time at work and too little with people she cared about. And whom did she really care about?

Of course, she loved her mom and siblings. But who else had she let inside her life?

Sobs racked her shoulders.

"Make her shut up," the driver said.

Chapter Nineteen

"What the hell do you mean they got her?" Reed fisted his hands as he glared at Luke. Their plane wouldn't land for another hour. "Have all airports and security checkpoints at the border been sealed?"

"Yes. And for what it's worth, I'm sorry, little bro." Anguish darkened Luke's eyes. "As you know, there are only a few places they can cross the border—"

"Legally. But this guy has more channels than cable TV." Whatever they'd done to Emily before would be nothing compared with the torture they'd dish out now. Reed cursed.

"I just spoke to the pilot. Our flight has been diverted to Laredo. There are only so many routes they can take to get to the border."

"That's true." Reed thought about it long and hard. Which highway in Texas would they take? Or was that too easy? "He expects everyone to be watching for him in Texas, so he won't risk it. Can you talk to the pilot, have him take us to El Paso instead?"

"I'm on it," Luke said as he made a move toward the cabin.

Reed leaned back in his seat and tried to stem the onset of a raging headache.

"We'll find her." The determination in Nick's eyes almost convinced Reed.

EMILY HAD NO idea how long they'd been driving when she heard a harsh word grunted and the screech of a hard brake. The van careened out of control and into a dangerous spin.

The next thing she knew, the van was in a death roll. The man who'd been sitting on top of her acted as a cushion, sparing her head from slamming against the ceiling now beneath them.

Emily braced herself as the van stopped. If she could get to the door while everyone was disoriented, maybe she could get away and make a run for it. She doubted there'd be anyone around to help since she hadn't heard a car pass by in hours.

She made a move to grab the handle. The Hispanic man caught her arm.

"Where do you think you're going?" he asked.

The door flew open, anyway, and there he stood. Reed. His gun was aimed at a spot on the Hispanic guy's head. Six other officers stood to each side of him.

"She's coming with me, Cal. And you're going to jail." Satisfaction lightened Reed's intense features.

Cal? The man who'd shot Reed?

Emily leaned toward him, unable to get her bearings enough to make her legs move. Or maybe they were broken because they didn't seem to want to move.

Dozens of officers moved on the men in the van, subduing them while Emily was being hauled into Reed's arms.

"I thought I lost you." The anguish in his voice nearly ripped out her heart.

"You can't get rid of me that easily, Campbell." She wrapped her arms around his neck.

He tightened his arms around her. "How badly are you hurt?"

"I'm shaken up, but I'll be okay." She tested her legs. Much to her relief, they worked fine. Adrenaline was fading, causing her to shake harder. Glancing around, all she could see was barren land. "Where am I?"

"In New Mexico. About five minutes from the Mexican border."

Reed held her so close she could hear his heart beat as wildly as her own. Relief flooded her.

"And that's the guy who shot you?" She motioned toward Cal.

"Yeah."

"I understand if you want to be the one to cuff him."

"I'm exactly where I want to be."

"And your brothers?"

"They're following a car we believe Dueño is in. We've been watching the caravan for an hour, waiting for it to split up so we could make a move. I knew Dueño wouldn't risk drawing too much attention so close to the border. He spread his men out and we made our move." His cell buzzed. He fished it from his pocket, keeping one arm secure around her waist, and then glanced from the screen to her. "It's Luke."

Reed said a few uh-huhs into the phone before ending the call. "Dueño got away. And they can't find him. Knox was driving. He's under arrest."

A helicopter roared toward them, hovering over him. If the officers shot it down, innocent lives would be lost. Reed tucked Emily behind him and moved to cover.

The chopper landed in a field, kicking up a tornado of dust.

"I have to distract him or he'll get away."

Reed caught Emily's elbow as she tried to pass him. His anger nearly scorched her skin. "I won't let you do this."

"It's the only way. If I can get him out in the open, maybe one of the guys can get a shot."

"A man who hides behind women and children won't risk being exposed." Reed stepped in between Emily and the chopper, weapon leveled and ready.

Movement to her left caught Emily's eye. She made a move to let Reed know, but his gun had already been redirected.

"Stop moving and put your hands where I can see them," Reed demanded.

"Put down your weapon and I'll consider it," Dueño said. The sound of his voice sent an icy chill down Emily's back.

"Always looking for the advantage, aren't you?"

"What would you do if you were in my position?"

"That's where you're wrong. I'm nothing like you. I'd never be in your position."

Dueño spun toward them, a flash of metal in his hand.

Fire exploded from Reed's gun first. Dueño took a few steps toward them, and then dropped to the ground. SWAT had already mobilized, taking down the pilot.

"We did it," Emily said. Relief and joy filled her soul as Reed's arms wrapped around her, pulling her body flush with his.

"You're safe now."

"When they abducted me, my worst fear wasn't dying. It was that I'd never see you again. I love you, Reed. I want to be with you, even though I know you'll never fully trust anyone who isn't a Campbell." She'd said it, and the heaviness on her chest released. Like a butterfly breaking free from its cocoon, flapping its wings for the very first time. He didn't have to say it back for happiness to engulf her. She loved him. And she wanted him to know.

His intense gaze pierced her for a long moment. "We can change that, you know."

"Change what?" she parroted.

"Your last name." Holding her gaze, right there, he bent down on one knee.

"I've always been a logical man, believing everything had a place and a time, and had to make sense. Until the day I met you. From that moment, I knew there was something different about you. I was in love. I love you. And the only thing that makes sense to me now is to grab hold with both hands, and hang on with everything I have. Will you do me the honor of becoming my wife?"

Tears of joy streamed down Emily's face as she said the one word she knew Reed needed to hear. "Yes."

"I've been talking about it with my brothers and we've decided to open a P.I. business together in Creek Bend. I want to be around for you. And I promise to love and protect you for the rest of my life." He rose to his feet, never breaking eye contact, and pulled her into a warm embrace.

In his arms, Emily had found her permanent family, she'd found exactly where she belonged. She'd found home.

* * * * *

COMING NEXT MONTH FROM

⬧ HARLEQUIN

INTRIGUE

Available February 17, 2015

**YOU CAN FIND MORE INFORMATION ON UPCOMING HARLEQUIN® TITLES,
FREE EXCERPTS AND MORE AT WWW.HARLEQUIN.COM.**

HICNM0215

REQUEST YOUR FREE BOOKS!
2 FREE NOVELS PLUS 2 FREE GIFTS!

⬥ HARLEQUIN

INTRIGUE

BREATHTAKING ROMANTIC SUSPENSE

YES! Please send me 2 FREE Harlequin Intrigue® novels and my 2 FREE gifts (gifts are worth about $10). After receiving them, if I don't wish to receive any more books, I can return the shipping statement marked "cancel." If I don't cancel, I will receive 6 brand-new novels every month and be billed just $4.74 per book in the U.S. or $5.24 per book in Canada. That's a savings of at least 14% off the cover price! It's quite a bargain! Shipping and handling is just 50¢ per book in the U.S. and 75¢ per book in Canada.* I understand that accepting the 2 free books and gifts places me under no obligation to buy anything. I can always return a shipment and cancel at any time. Even if I never buy another book, the two free books and gifts are mine to keep forever.

182/382 HDN F42N

Name	(PLEASE PRINT)	
Address		Apt. #
City	State/Prov.	Zip/Postal Code

Signature (if under 18, a parent or guardian must sign)

Mail to the **Harlequin® Reader Service:**
IN U.S.A.: P.O. Box 1867, Buffalo, NY 14240-1867
IN CANADA: P.O. Box 609, Fort Erie, Ontario L2A 5X3
**Are you a subscriber to Harlequin Intrigue books
and want to receive the larger-print edition?
Call 1-800-873-8635 or visit www.ReaderService.com.**

* Terms and prices subject to change without notice. Prices do not include applicable taxes. Sales tax applicable in N.Y. Canadian residents will be charged applicable taxes. Offer not valid in Quebec. This offer is limited to one order per household. Not valid for current subscribers to Harlequin Intrigue books. All orders subject to credit approval. Credit or debit balances in a customer's account(s) may be offset by any other outstanding balance owed by or to the customer. Please allow 4 to 6 weeks for delivery. Offer available while quantities last.

Your Privacy—The Harlequin® Reader Service is committed to protecting your privacy. Our Privacy Policy is available online at www.ReaderService.com or upon request from the Harlequin Reader Service.

We make a portion of our mailing list available to reputable third parties that offer products we believe may interest you. If you prefer that we not exchange your name with third parties, or if you wish to clarify or modify your communication preferences, please visit us at www.ReaderService.com/consumerchoice or write to us at Harlequin Reader Service Preference Service, P.O. Box 9062, Buffalo, NY 14269. Include your complete name and address.

HI13R

A Texas deputy steps in to protect a vulnerable witness, even though she could send his own father to jail...

"You know that I'm staying here with you tonight, right," Colt said when he pulled to a stop in front of her house.

Elise was certain that wasn't a question, and she wanted to insist his babysitting her wasn't necessary.

But she was afraid that it was.

Because someone wanted her dead. Had even sent someone to end her life. And that someone had nearly succeeded.

She'd hoped the bone-deep exhaustion would tamp down the fear. It didn't. She was feeling both fear and fatigue, and that wasn't a good mix.

Nor was having Colt around.

However, the alternative was her being alone in her house that was miles from town or her nearest neighbor. And for just the rest of the night, she wasn't ready for the alone part. In the morning though, she would have to do something to remedy it. Something that didn't include Colt and her under the same roof.

For now though, that was exactly what was about to happen.

They got out of his truck, the sleet still spitting at them, and the air so bitterly cold that it burned her lungs with each breath she took. Elise's hands were still shaking, and when she tried to unlock the front door of her house, she dropped the gob of keys, the metal sound clattering onto the weathered wood porch. Colt reached for them at the same time she did, and their heads ended up colliding.

Right on her stitches.

The pain shot through her, and even though Elise tried to choke back the groan, she didn't quite succeed.

"Sorry." Colt cursed and snatched the keys from her to unlock the door. He definitely wasn't shaking.

"Wait here," he ordered the moment they stepped into the living room. He shut the door, gave her a stay-put warning glance and drew his gun before he started looking around.

Only then did Elise realize that someone—another hit man maybe—could be already hiding inside. Waiting to kill her.

Sweet heaven.

When was this going to end?

As the threats to Elise Nichols escalate, so does the tension between her and sexy cowboy Colt McKinnon!

Don't miss their heart-stopping story when
THE DEPUTY'S REDEMPTION,
part of USA TODAY *bestselling author*
Delores Fossen's **SWEETWATER RANCH** *miniseries,*
goes on sale in March 2015.

JUST CAN'T GET ENOUGH
ROMANCE
Looking for more?

Harlequin has everything from contemporary, passionate and heartwarming to suspenseful and inspirational stories.

Whatever your mood, we have a romance just for you!

Connect with us to find your next great read, special offers and more.

Facebook.com/HarlequinBooks
Twitter.com/HarlequinBooks
HarlequinBlog.com
Harlequin.com/Newsletters

A *Romance* FOR EVERY MOOD™

www.Harlequin.com